ADORABLE FAT GIRL GOES TO WEIGHT LOSS CAMP

BERNICE BLOOM

CONTENTS

CHAPTER ONE: NOTHING BUT CARROTS

I was all curled up on mum's sofa, clutching a sweet cup of tea and feeling its warmth against the palms of my hands, as rain hammered against the windows. It had been pouring all day and was now coming down so hard that you could hear it hitting the conservatory roof like gunfire. Darkness had started to descend. It was only 7pm for God's sake. Outside it looked like the end of the world.

"I should go home soon," I said. "But this rain is just awful. I can't face going out in it."

"No, don't be ridiculous. You can't go anywhere til it stops. Just relax and enjoy your tea. Stay for something to eat and your dad will run you back later."

"Thanks mum," I said, snuggling further down into the sofa and feeling all safe and secure. The theme tune for the One Show came on and I don't think I'd ever felt cosier in my life. I clutched my mug between my hands and blew onto the scalding liquid, watching the steam fly up onto my face, warming my nose. It was like I was giving myself a mini steam facial.

"How are things going then?" asked mum, eying me with

confusion as I tried to get the steam to hit my chin where I'm particularly prone to blackheads. "What on earth are you trying to do with that mug?"

"Nothing," I said, continuing to hold the mug in position. You'd pay £40 for this sort of treatment at the beauticians.

"You seem a bit out of sorts. Is everything OK with you and Ted?"

I shrugged, not because things weren't going well with my boyfriend, but because I now had my chin right over the top of the mug and didn't want to move.

"For the love of God, are you having some sort of break-down over there? Or are you trying to drink your tea through your chin?"

"Neither," I said, reluctantly putting down the mug. "I was just warming up my chin."

"Warming up your chin?"

"Yes. My chin was cold, that's all." I crossed my arms over my chest and turned to watch the television. They had just started a segment about window boxes.

"You and Ted aren't getting on well, are you?" she said, her voice full of anxiety. "He's such a lovely man, it would be a shame if you messed this up."

"Things are fine," I replied, turning my attention back to the planting taking place in the BBC studio. "He works long hours and I've been away a lot recently, so we haven't seen all that much of one another, but everything's just fine."

"Oh," she said. "Doesn't sound like things are 'just fine' if you never see him. And 'fine' is such an odd word to use. I thought you two were in love."

"We are. Honestly, mum, we're both doing really well and the relationship's great, I just want to see what they do with these primroses."

"OK," she said, taking a large gulp of tea, but she looked far from OK. She clearly wanted to talk but I genuinely wanted to see what they would put next to the primroses. I work in a gardening and DIY store, and I have been charged with sorting out all the window boxes next week. I needed tips from Alan Titchmarsh.

Mum fell into a respectful silence while the colourful, floral creations took shape. Then the programme moved onto Phil Tufnell talking about the plight of urban foxes. Mum seized her moment and grabbed the remote control, hitting the pause button and leaving poor Phil frozen on the screen. I knew what was coming.

"Come on then," she said. "Tell me what the trouble is."

"There's no trouble. Honestly, mum. Ted and I are very happy."

"But there's no talk of you moving in together? No talk of wedding bells?"

"No talk like that at all, mum. But we're happy so stop worrying."

"I do worry, I can't help it," she said. "You were always so sad and out of sorts until Ted came along...he's transformed you. He's a lovely man. I'd hate to see things going wrong."

"They won't. Everything's fine. Now can we talk about something else, or I'll put the foxes back on."

"OK. You can talk to me anytime you want, if you're worried about anything."

"I know," I said. "And I will if I'm worried about anything." Although the one thing I'm absolutely sure of is that my mother would be the last person on the planet I'd talk to if I was having problems with my relationship.

"What are you up to, then?" she asked. "Any exciting trips planned?"

"Well, Ted and I are talking about going to America in the summer. He's looking at what sort of holiday we could do. I fancy a road trip - you know - take in a lot of places all in one visit. Route 66 and all that."

"I thought you were going somewhere else as well," said mum. "Like a health place or something?"

"Yes, I'm off on a weight loss retreat in Portugal next week. I told you all about that."

"A weight loss retreat. That's right," she mused, offering me a chocolate biscuit. I took one, of course. Always better to discuss the merits of weight loss retreats while dunking heavily-coated chocolate hobnobs into devilishly sweet tea.

"All they'll give you to eat at weight loss retreats is carrots. You do know that, don't you?"

"I'm sure that's not ALL we'll be given," I replied. "I'm sure there'll be other food."

"Nope...carrot juice, carrots in salads and carrots on their own - carrots lying on the plate in front of you, taunting you with their orangeness. By the end of the week you'll be having nightmares about carrots taking over the country. Just talk to Aunty Susan, she went on a Fat Camp when she was 20, before her wedding, and she was definitely a light orangey colour when she came home. Take a look at the wedding photos. Looks like Donald Trump, she does."

"She does not. I've seen her wedding photos, she looks lovely in them."

"Lovely, yes, but apricot coloured. I mean, apricot's a nice colour for a blouse or a summer skirt, but not for your face. In the wedding photos she looked like she's been living too close to a nuclear plant or been bathing in cheesy wotsits or something."

"Well, even if it was all about carrots back then, it's not now. Also, it's definitely not called 'Fat Camp'. You're talking about something from the 1950s, it's all different today. I'm going on a weight loss retreat and will have healthy food, fresh air and exercise and I'll come back energised and looking a lot like Jennifer Lawrence. It will be brilliant."

"Do you have to write about it again on that blog thing?"

"Yep," I said. "Another free trip."

I've got myself a nice little gig writing for my friend Dawn's blog. It's called 'Two Fat Ladies' and because I'm rather well-upholstered she invites me to help her review various holidays, The trouble is - things always go wrong.

This is the third trip I've managed to wangle myself onto. I've been on safari (got stuck up a tree in my knickers and it all ended up on webcam - disaster!) and went on a cruise (befriended a 90-year-old man and a flamboyant dancer and managed to miss the ship and bump into an ex-boyfriend - disaster!).

I'm hoping that this one will be straightforward and I'll come back looking thin and lovely without having created any colossal dramas along the way.

"Well I hope you're right. I hope that fat camps have changed since your Aunty Susan went," said mum, with a raise of her eyebrows. A smile played upon her lips and a look of furtive shame crept across her features. "It was funny though, hearing all the stories. I remember Susan telling me about when she escaped and went running to the pub with one of the other women, and the pub landlord guessed what they'd done and called the Fat Camp owner who sent out two guys to collect them and bring them back. They were even frisked back at Fat Club and two packets of pork scratchings were found in your Aunty Susan's knickers. Don't tell her I told you that though, will you? We called her piggy pants for ages after-wards...don't tell her I told you that either."

I smiled as I thought about my sensible aunty having pub snacks hidden in her girdle.

"I won't be like that," I said. "I want to go and do it properly and lose loads of weight so I can start on a proper health and fitness drive and really get down to a healthy, sensible weight."

"Good girl," said mum. "You won't want another one of these, then."

Mum took a hob nob and bit into it slowly, while I flicked through the weight loss camp brochure.

"Most people lose 7lbs on the holiday," I read out.

"That'll be the carrots," she replied through a mouth full of biscuit. I ignored her and carried on reading.

"If you join the running group you can expect to dramatically increase the speed and distance you can run."

"Yep, everyone running away from carrots," she said.

"There's no mention of bloody carrots in the brochure. They talk about healthy, organic food that will fill you up and give you the strength you need to exercise while allowing you to shed all the weight you want."

"The carrots are a secret."

"For the love of God, mum. Shut up about the carrots."

A week later, Aunty Susan came over for lunch with Uncle Mark and I knew the subject of my pending Weight Loss holiday would be raised. Mum was dying to have her theories about the holiday confirmed.

"I was telling Mary about the Fat Camp that you went on before your wedding, Sue," she said.

"Oh God!" said Aunty Susan, dropping her cutlery so it clattered on her plate. "That was terrible. Do you remember? Me and that other lady tried to escape but they came and caught us."

"I never knew about that," said Mark. "Where did you try to escape to?"

"To the pub and the fish and chip shop," replied Susan. "They caught us in the pub, I think, before we'd even had the chance to get to the fish and chip shop."

"Why would you try to escape?" Mark asked. "I thought you liked going to spas and things like that."

I braced myself.

"I love spas, but this place was dreadful...they made us exercise from 5am til 8pm, and fed us nothing but carrots."

"You see," said mum, turning around to face me with a look of triumph on her face. "What did I tell you? Nothing but carrots."

CHAPTER TWO: MUM ON TOUR

hile mum sat and explained to Aunty Susan how she'd been warning me about the carrots, my phone rang. Dawn's number appeared on the screen, so I excused myself and wandered into the kitchen.

"Hi Flairy, zits fawn," said Dawn's familiar voice.

"Sorry? I couldn't understand a word of that."

I could hear mum and Aunty Susan laughing uproariously as they were telling Uncle Mark all about the Fat Camp she'd been on. I noticed that they didn't mention her hiding pork scratchings in her knickers though. I must make sure to mention that.

"It's Fawn," said the voice on the phone.

"Fawn?"

"No, Dawn. Sorry - I've got a mouthful of food."

"Not carrots, I hope."

"No, of course not. I'm eating cake. Why would you think I'd be eating carrots?"

"Just something my mum was saying earlier about everyone at weight loss Camp eating nothing but carrots."

"Well, your mum will be able to find out for herself if she wants," said Dawn.

"What do you mean?"

"I mean she will literally be able to find out for herself. The organisers of the weight loss camp say you can take your mum with you because they are keen to advertise a Mother's' Day special that they are running next month. They thought that would make an interesting angle for the blog and I agree with them to be honest. You know 'weight loss camp with my mum'. I think it could be really funny for readers."

I was silent. I wasn't expecting this at all.

"Mary, are you still there?" asked Dawn.

"Yes, still here, but shocked into silence," I said. "I can't take my mum with me."

"Come on, it would make great copy. Can you imagine it… you're really witty, Mary, and have got yourself a great following already. Weight watching with your mum will add a whole new dimension to that. Readers will love it. Readers will think it's really funny as they hear all about the two of you."

"Yeah, funny for readers, but hell on earth for me."

"I'm sure your mum is lovely."

"She is," I said, as mum walked past me to get more drink. She pulled out a fresh bottle of sherry and I realised they were in for a long night…when she and Aunty Susan get cracking on the sherry there's no stopping them: they'll be dancing to Elvis and Buddy Holly in no time. "But mum's not fat. I can't take my mum on a weight loss camp if she doesn't need to lose weight, that would be crazy."

"Oooooooo…" said mum, stopping in the doorway with her bottle of sherry and spinning round to face me. "Yes, you can take me to weight loss camp with you. I definitely need to lose a few pounds," she said. "Everyone over the age of 60 needs to lose weight. I used to be so slim and elegant. Not anymore though. Take me with you, Mary, we'd have such fun."

"Let me talk this through with her and I'll come back to you" I said to Dawn, as I ended the call and followed mum into the sitting room. Mum was in there flexing her muscles at Aunty Susan. She had rolled up the short sleeves of her silk top and was displaying arms with the merest hint of flabby skin hanging beneath them. This was supposed to indicate how overweight she was.

"Isn't it awful," she was saying to Aunty Susan, as she gently nudged her arm and shook her head as it rippled. "However slim you keep yourself, you can't help it when you get older.

"I wouldn't worry, mum, I've got more loose flesh than that on my ankles," I said.

"So, am I coming?"

"I don't think it will be your sort of thing," I tried. "I mean - when have you ever shown any interest in health and fitness?"

"Excuse me, Madam, but when have you?" asked mum.

I nodded at her. She had a point. Though, in my defence, I do talk a lot about getting fit...I just don't do anything about it. Does it count if you talk about it endlessly?

"I took up yoga," I said, remembering my weekend retreat a while ago. "I wore nothing but bloody Lycra for days."

"Well, that's true," said mum. "But how much yoga did you actually do? It sounds to me like you spent most of the time falling over and ogling men in tight shorts."

Again, she wasn't wrong.

"I think it would be lovely if we went to the weight loss camp together. I mean, I understand if you say you don't want me to go with you, but I'd really like to."

"Ah, go on Mary, take her," said Aunty Susan. "She'll be very well-behaved."

Oh God, why was this so hard?

"But remember what you said about the carrots," I said.

"You wouldn't want to have to eat carrots for every meal, would you?"

"I wouldn't mind," said mum. "I wouldn't mind what I ate as long as I was with you."

Bugger, bugger, bugger. What could I possibly say to that?

"Of course I'd like you to come, mum," I told her, with a heavy heart. I'd imagined myself frolicking on the beach with handsome instructors and flirting outrageously with the tennis coaches before sneaking out for late night glasses of wine with the other guests, not to mention the snacks I was planning to take. Now it looked like it was going to be all fitness classes and games of Scrabble.

"Ooo, what fun," mum said. "Don't worry about a thing now, Mary. I'll be there to keep you on the straight and narrow and out of trouble."

"That's what I'm worried about," I said.

It was five days to go before the weight loss retreat and I was trying so hard to be good. I didn't want to look like a pot-bellied pig in my bikini. Going with mum added a whole new level of stress to the trip; she was so lovely and slim - I didn't want everyone to be looking at us both and wondering why on earth I was so huge when she was so tiny. I thought that at least if I lay off the booze and cut back on the snacks I'd look a bit better...just a bit.

"I'm not going to drink tonight," I said to Ted, refusing a glass, and taking a sip of his wine when his back was turned. "I'm going to be good."

"Um..." said Ted, having seen me stealing his glass out of the corner of his eye. "For someone who's not going to drink tonight you seem to be drinking a hell of a lot of my wine."

"Everyone knows that calories taken off someone else's plate or from someone else's glass don't count," I advised.

"Right," said Ted, looking highly dubious.

"It's a flawless plan, to be fair," I said, taking another large sip from his glass.

"Just have a glass of wine if you want glass of wine, woman." he said. "You're not going to get any fatter drinking your own glass instead of my glass."

God love him; does he know nothing?

"By the way, what are you doing tomorrow? Do you fancy coming to the football with me?" he said. "There's a group of us going, it will be a laugh."

"I'd rather sit at home and stick pins in my eyes - why would I want to go to the football?"

"All the other girlfriends go," he said in whiny voice. "They talk among themselves, you don't have to watch the football...just come along and have a beer and mix with everyone."

"Next time," I said. "I'm going holiday shopping with mum tomorrow to get supplies for our trip." Heaven help me; I'm not sure which is the worse day out - football with Ted and his lager lout friends or clothes shopping with mum.

"Blimey, are you sure you wouldn't rather come to the football?"

"I have to go with her," I said. "If I don't it will be an utter disaster. Yesterday she was talking about buying a jazzy pink headband and ankle warmers to wear to the fitness classes. If I don't take her in hand she'll look like Jane Fonda's grandmother. I need to go with her to make sure she doesn't lose her mind in Sports Direct."

"OK, well - rather you than me - if you change your mind, come down to the football - you know where we'll be."

"I will," I said.

The next day I woke with a heavy heart at the thought of the delights ahead of me. My mum is lovely, she really is, and I'm sure your mum is too, but would you want to go on holiday with her? Honestly? And would you want to go shopping for fitness wear with her in advance of the holiday? You don't need to answer that; we all know the answer.

I caught the bus over to mum's house in Esher first thing in the morning and picked her up, then the two of us went on the bus into Kingston. She was so chirpy and thrilled at the idea of going shopping with me that I felt really bad for all the things I'd been thinking. I decided to be positive and upbeat and make this whole experience something that mum would love.

"Where shall we go first?" asked mum. Her cheeks were all flushed and she looked really excited that we were out on a shopping trip. I swear, you'd think I never went anywhere with her, or that she had never been shopping before. "I suppose you'll want to go to Topshop or Zara - or some of those other young person's shops, won't you?" she said. "I'll come with you, but will need to get my clothes somewhere a little more age-appropriate."

I didn't want to tell mum that the clothes in Topshop hadn't fitted me since puberty, and I hadn't been in Zara since I got stuck in a dress there and ended up ripping it in an effort to get it off.

"I was thinking about the department stores - John Lewis and Bentalls, and maybe Marks and Spencer," I said. I knew they were the most likely shops to stock a swimming costume that was big enough for me. I also needed a cover-all kaftan so I didn't scare the locals and a summery dress in case there was a cocktail party one evening. "Do those shops sound OK?"

"Yes, very nice," she said, looking delighted with my suggestions. "And we don't have to worry about paying for lunch because I've bought sandwiches with me." She opened her bag to reveal cling film wrapped bread at the bottom, and a flask."

"That's soup in there. It's Heinz so it should be nice. And

I've got boiled eggs for us to have with the sandwiches. They're here, somewhere."

"Great," I said, as mum rummaged around on her egg hunt. "We'll go to the park after shopping for a picnic."

Mum brightened further at the thought of that.

We decided to go to Sports Direct first, mainly because we walked right past it when we got off the bus, but also because mum wanted trainers and dad had persuaded her that the only decent place to buy trainers was a sports shop.

"Your father says that I mustn't buy cheap ones from a supermarket, I've got to buy proper ones from a sports shop or I'll slip and break my hip or something."

"OK," I said, and in we went. Mum tried on a succession of shoes and as she skipped around the shop, testing them out, I thought how youthful she looked - she was very young-looking for her age and didn't have an ounce of fat on her.

"I think I'll take these pink ones," she said, with a girlish smile. "Shall I get you some too?"

"I'd look ridiculous in them," I said. "I only wear black trainers."

"Well, I think you should get some brightly coloured ones. You'd look lovely in these."

"No mum, honestly, it's really kind of you, but last time I wore pink I look like Tinky Winky so I've stopped all bright colours until I lose weight."

"Let me buy you something," said mum. "Choose whatever you fancy as a treat from me."

I didn't want to buy anything in the sports shop. Nothing looks more ridiculous than a woman who's clearly not done a moment's exercise since the 1990s, all dressed up in brand new exercise gear, especially if the gear is three sizes too small…. which it would have been if I'd attempted to buy something in there.

After the shoe shopping, we went upstairs and mum

bought some very lovely, deeply-flattering Lycra sportswear. I can't tell you how annoying it is when your mum looks better in clothes than you do. I could have hit her as she emerged from the changing rooms saying: "Could you get one of these for me in a size 10, Mary? This one's far too big for me."

As I watched her, I kept thinking 'why am I fat, and she's not?' I mean - how does the whole overeating thing work? Surely, you'd think that I would be fat because my mum is fat, and she over fed me from a young age, or gave me a negative relationship with food, or something. But it doesn't seem to work like that - I seem to be unable to stop eating and unable to stop thinking about eating, whereas mum just eats when she's hungry.

Our relationships with food are so different. It's like food means a different thing in both our lives - to me it's a joyous thing hovering on the horizon, never quite out of sight, always alluring and always exciting. When there's food in the room it's like I become a person possessed...I can't relax til it's all eaten, and when I eat it it's like I can't get enough of it, like there's no amount of food that's ever going to satisfy me, ever going to fill me up and allow me to relax. I just wish I didn't have to eat ever again. I wish eating wasn't part of life.

"Right," said mum, returning to me with all her purchases packed away in a carrier bag. "Let's go and have a picnic in the park, shall we?"

"Oooh yes," I said, trotting along beside her, my maudlin mood lifted a little by the thought of food (see what I mean? It's insane).

"Shall we walk down to the grassy bank that we went past on the bus a little earlier? It seemed nice there, didn't it?"

"Or we could go just here," I said, indicating a small park that was not as nice as the spot that mum was talking about, but was nearer, meaning we could eat sooner and I wouldn't have to walk for ages.

"I thought the spot by the river was nicer?"

"No - the ducks and geese come there and they're really vicious," I said. "This will be much better." I threw down my coat as a makeshift blanket before mum could attempt to make me change my mind.

"OK," she said, and started unloading the picnic. I felt instantly bad for making her sit there. I'm just horrible when there's food around.

"We can go back to the river if you like," I said.

"No, said mum, opening a very small packet of sandwiches. "Don't worry. This is just perfect."

CHAPTER THREE: SOLDIERING ALONG

The flight left on a Monday, while Ted was at work, so the task of taking two women and bags full of leisurewear to the airport fell to dad.

"Now have you both definitely got everything," he said, once we were in the car with our luggage in the boot. "Check now, before we leave."

We both rummaged through our respective handbags and said we were OK. We had our passports with us and that's all that mattered.

"You don't need tickets?" asked dad.

"Err no - it's all magic now," I said. "They are e-tickets - on my phone."

"Have you got the information about the camp and how we get there?" asked mum.

I pulled an envelope out of my bag. "All in here," I said. I hadn't opened it, but I knew it was all there. With that we were off - chugging along the motorway on our journey to Heathrow.

. . .

After checking in and passing through security with an alarming lack of hassle or incident, mum and I headed for the beauty counters in the duty-free shop.

I sprayed a liberal amount of Chanel No5 onto my wrists and neck and tipped way too much body lotion into my hands so that I ended up spreading it all the way up my arms to get rid of it. Mum was peering into a small mirror at the skin care counter next to me, wrinkling up her nose in disgust at the sight of herself. "You've no idea how bloody hideous it is," she said.

"How hideous what is, mum?" I replied. The lipstick she'd tried on seemed perfectly acceptable to me.

"Ageing... Waking up in the morning and discovering that your jawline has drop so far that your jowls are resting on your shoulders, and your eyes have disappeared completely – hidden behind bags, wrinkles and a forehead that's dropped four inches."

I should tell you at this stage that mum is really attractive; she is slim, elegant and always has perfect hair (You know how some people are like that... They always have the most gorgeous hair, where is mine is hit and miss – regardless of what I do with it, sometimes it looks okay and other times it looks terrible for no reason at all).

Anyway – what I'm saying is mum looks good, and she's not all that vain, so the small outburst as she peered into the mirror came as a bit of a shock.

"You look great mum, what are you talking about?"

"I'm talking about the unwanted hairs popping up on my chin, the grey roots and the beachball that has appeared where my waistline used to be. The only thing I've got in my favour is that I haven't got incontinence or piles, unlike Aunty Susan."

"Yeah, thanks mum. I really needed to know that."

"And the reason for that is because I do daily pelvic floor exercises and it makes the world of difference. You should start now. I'll show you when we get to the room. Honestly, I do them so often it's a wonder I can't get my pelvic floor up to touch the back of my throat."

"Oh God, mum."

I turned to look at the mascaras. My eyes are the only part of me that I like. I have big eyes, you see. In fact, I have big everything, but big eyes are allowed. Have you ever thought about that? I have really big feet and that's frowned upon. Having size eight feet is not ladylike. Having big thighs is not good and neither is having a big tummy. But big eyes? That's good; that's allowed. A big smile is allowed too, but not a big neck.

I need to go and live in a country where all big is beautiful and my huge arse is celebrated as much as my huge eyes. Maybe Tonga or somewhere. Isn't the King of Tonga chosen as king because he's the fattest person in the country? Christ, I'd be running the place in the blink of an eye.

I turned back to mum to find her holding her forehead up with her index fingers so that her eyebrows were raised, and she was pulling the sides of her face out with her thumbs.

"Do I look young?" she asked.

I didn't know what the right answer was. If I said "yes" that would imply that I thought she looked old normally, but if I said "No" then she'd think that even when she rearranged her features with her fingers, she still looked old.

"You look startled," I told her. "Not a good look, if you don't mind me saying. Now come on, let's go and get a drink. I want to tell you about all my plans to move to Tonga."

It was only a swift visit to the pub (mum wasn't such a fan of all day drinking as I'd hoped she'd be), then I rushed into Boots and bought more miniature toiletry items than either of us could reasonably get through in a decade, as well as stocking up on medical supplies for the flight in such quantities that we could have opened a small on-board hospital. Then it was time to board.

On the plane, I settled myself into my seat and nervously raised my hand to attract the attention of the attendant.

"Can I help you?" she asked in a loud voice.

"I'll need a seatbelt extension please," I said.

"A what?"

"A seat belt extender," I said, doing actions to mimic the putting on of a seatbelt rather than raise my voice.

"Of course, madam," she said, scurrying off to find one.

"You don't need a seatbelt extender," said mum, valiantly rushing to my defence. "You're not that fat."

I love that she's so protective, but her loyalty is verging on blindness. The seat-belt extender only just goes around me.

"Shall we have a little drink on the plane?" I suggested.

"Tea?" she said.

"Gin?" I responded.

"Are you an alcoholic?" she asked.

"What? Because I fancy a little drink on the plane on the way to holiday?"

"No, because it's a weight loss camp and only a nutcase would order alcohol on the way to it…. a nutter, or someone who loved drinking so much they couldn't help themselves. Someone with a problem, perhaps?"

"It's going to be a long five days," I muttered under my breath, as we both ordered tea. "A long, long time."

We arrived at Faro airport and I pulled the letter out of my bag to work out where we were supposed to be. I slid my finger along the seal and tore the envelope open, pulling out the pages inside.

"Let's see, it's called... 'Forces Fitness'," I said, noticing the military-style logo at the top of the information sheet.

"Forces fitness?" said mum. "What do you mean? Like military training? Drill sergeants and press ups in the mud?"

Mum and I looked at one another.

"Forces Fitness? Shit," I said. "I thought it would be all fruit kebabs and sparkling elderflower juice. I don't fancy military fitness at all."

"It can't be," said mum. "Was there information with the letter? What does it say?"

"I didn't really look," I confessed, flicking through all the other pages in the envelope which announced that the camp was a military style fitness experience.

"Oh God...look mum."

Two men dressed in army fatigues were marching up to us, clutching clipboards. One of them was around my age and desperately handsome with chiselled features and big shoulders. He looked tough and manly but he also had long eyelashes and sea green eyes. He looked as if he could handle himself in a fight, but would also be nice to kittens and always remember your birthday. The other man was older and looked as if he would crush kittens with his bare hands and force feed them to you on your birthday. It was odd because the younger man was bigger and much stronger-looking, but somehow had a warmth about him that was lacking in his mate. The older man snarled at me.

"Names?" he said as if I was a prisoner who'd just been captured. I felt like turning around and running back through security and onto the plane and demanding that it take me right back to London. I couldn't face this week if it comprised of them shouting and calling me useless and hopeless in an effort to break me down. I'm broken enough, I need building not breaking, for God's sake.

"Didn't you hear me?" he said. "I need your names and I need your passports to be surrendered."

"OK, well I'm Mary and this is my mum," I replied, directing my comment to the handsome man. "And why do we have to 'surrender' our passports, are we being arrested or something?"

"Passports," he said.

Mum obediently rummaged in her handbag to find hers, but I wasn't interested in playing their silly games.

"I've told you our names, what are yours?"

"Staff A and Staff B," replied the man, adding: "We don't do first names."

Oh God.

"Look, we only want to lose a few pounds. Neither of us is planning to invade anywhere and we have no desire to fight anyone. I just want a nice relaxing week."

"OK Mary," he said, putting his face right next to mine in quite a threatening way. "We'll see what we can do. Follow me."

Mum and I half-walked, half-skipped behind the two men who strode out in front. The only compensatory factor was that the handsome man (who I think was Staff B) had the most incredible tight bum.

I could see that mum was struggling beside me. She did a little run to keep up and moved her bag from one hand to the other. He could have offered to carry it for her. I mean - I know they're doing this whole 'tough guy' thing, but mum's not far off 70, for God's sake.

I took the bag out of mum's hand and carried it along with my own, struggling to keep up with them as they marched ahead. Then a very tall man appeared beside me. He was long and lean with round glasses and a mop of sandy blond hair

"Let me take that," he said, relieving me of mum's bag. He

had a warm, friendly face and looked a little shy - not at all like the other two guys.

"Do you work for the fitness camp," I asked, wondering why he wasn't all dressed up in army fatigues.

"No. I'm a guest," he said. "I'm Simon."

Oh, I see. "I'm Mary," I said, smiling at him. He had lovely warm eyes. There was something tender and likable about him. He wasn't conventionally good looking, but had charisma. When he smiled his whole face lit up. I noticed that mum had speeded up and was talking to the fearsome-looking army guys.

"So, are you looking forward to this week?" I asked him. "To be honest, I'm terrified of what they're going to get us doing. I didn't realise it was a military fitness thing. I thought it would be Slimming World in the sunshine."

"You'll be fine," he said with a small laugh. "I mean - it's not quite Slimming World but I'm sure you'll enjoy it. I've been on one of these camps before and they're good fun once you get going. Don't worry. These guys act tough but they're good at what they do, and if you listen to them, you'll lose a lot of weight and feel great by Friday."

I smiled at him adoringly and thought how much more fun this whole holiday would be now that I had someone to chat to and flirt a little with. Not that I fancied him...he just had a nice manner, and clearly liked me, which was lovely.

"Are you very fit?" I said. "If you don't mind me asking. I'm worried that I won't be fit enough to keep up."

"Not really," said Simon. "I cycle every day but I'm not super fit so don't worry. On a camp like this you'll find that there's always someone fitter than you and someone less fit than you."

I didn't imagine they'd find someone less fit than me, but I appreciated the comment, so I smiled happily at Simon and thanked him.

"Do you mind if I ask you something?" he said, looking a little embarrassed.

"Of course," I said, fluttering my eyelashes, delighted that I'd coated them in brown owl mascara at the airport.

"I'm always blunt when it comes to seeing a lady that I'm attracted to, I don't like to hang back."

"Oh," I said, feeling my heart beating a little faster. "OK then. What did you want to ask me?"

I knew he was going to ask whether I was single. I felt excited at the prospect, but what should I say? I was tempted to lie so that I could keep the magic alive between the two of us...it would make the week so much more fun if I had someone to flirt with. But it seemed really bad of me not to mention Ted.

"What I wanted to ask you was - who's that lady who was with you earlier, the one whose bag I'm carrying? She's really attractive."

What?

"THAT'S MY MUM!" I growled.

"Oh," he said. "Is your dad on the trip?"

"No," I replied. "But my mum and dad are still together, so keep your hands off her."

"OK," he said, looking a little shocked by my outburst. "But if your mum and dad ever split up, I'd be really interested."

"Get away from me," I said, making shooing motions at him. "Go on; go away."

My bloody mother! What the hell did it say for my attractiveness if men preferred my mum? Christ, this was going to be a marvellous few days.

CHAPTER FOUR: FOUR VILLAS IN THE SUNSHINE

We all climbed into the back of a small minibus. There was me, mum, Simon who I had completely gone off and was keen to keep as far from my mum as possible, and one of the army blokes (the handsome one). The older, angrier army guy had gone back to meet the rest of the group in his inimitable, gentle style. He arrived back a few minutes later with another couple of people: a woman called Karen and a guy called Graham.

Karen looked utterly terrified as she took her seat and looked up at the two army guys.

"They aren't as horrible as they look," I whispered to her, though I had no evidence for that - I just couldn't stand to see her looking so downcast and sad. She smiled weakly and muttered 'good', before turning to smile at mum.

"Sorry, I didn't catch your name," said Graham, so I introduced myself and mum and completely ignored Simon.

"What's your sports specialism?" said Graham.

What?

"Um. I don't really have one," I said. "I mean - I was a really good gymnast years ago, when I was young - but I wouldn't say I had a sports specialism now. Why? Are we supposed to have one?"

I looked at Staff B who was watching us with amusement from his position in the front seat. Despite the heat he had a long-sleeved shirt on and these white gloves. He must be boiling.

"No one needs any sort of specialty. We're planning to work you hard so you get the most out of the week but you won't have to do anything you don't want to. Please stop worrying."

"Does your angry-looking mate know that?" I asked. "Only he looks ready to waterboard us if we put a foot wrong."

"Don't mention waterboarding," said Staff B, suddenly getting very serious. "Never mention it. We've all been in the army, we've all experienced terrible things. Please - just don't mention it."

"OK," I said meekly, looking at mum. "Sorry."

"But in answer to your question - yes, my angry mate does know, and he's not expecting any sporting prowess either. And don't worry. His bark is worse than his bite."

"Phew," said Simon. "I don't have any particular sporting prowess. I don't know what I'd say my skills were."

"Fancying old ladies," I said under my breath, as Staff A reappeared at the side of the mini bus, looking concerned.

"I can't find her," he said.

"No, there's no one else coming," said Staff B. "We're all here. I've just checked the list. Shall we make a move?"

"No - there's someone else coming," said Staff A. "You know - the girl. I mentioned her."

"Of course," said Staff B. "Fucking hell, how could I forget. Go find her. I'll stay here." Then he turned back round to face us.

"We're just waiting for one other person to arrive," he said.

"She's coming on the Manchester flight. She'll be here any minute."

I turned my attention to mum, who'd gone very quiet.

"Everything OK?" I asked.

"Yes, just feeling a bit tired now. I could do with a nap. Travelling is exhausting when you're older."

"Have a little nap now," I suggested, bundling up my jumper and her coat behind her head so she could lean back on the window. I looked up to see Simon smiling at her. He swung his head away when he saw me looking.

Minutes later Staff A emerged from the airport building with a very glamorous brunette, strikingly slim in white jeans and white t-shirt with gold high-heeled sandals and a gorgeous lemon-coloured scarf around her neck. She looked stunning.

I noticed that Staff A was carrying her bag for her. Great. So, my ancient mother had to carry hers herself, but old skinny legs was given a helping hand. Immediately, for no reason at all, I got a sudden feeling that something was going on between Staff A and the glamorous brunette. Something about the way he was talking to her...leaning in so closely and smiling. It was the first time I'd seen him smile since we arrived.

And what was someone so skinny doing on a weight loss retreat in the first place? Why would she need to be here? It didn't add up.

He helped her into the minibus with such tenderness, it was like a scene from Love Story. "Everything OK?" he asked. "Just say if you need anything." Then he stroked her cheek gently and closed the doors.

"Let's go," he said to Staff B.

"I'm Yvonne," said the attractive lady and we all murmured greetings back to her as she made herself comfortable, taking up about 1 inch of space.

"Have you known Staff A long," I said.

"No, I've never met him before," she said.

"Oh, you two seemed so close. I assumed you were old friends."

"Nope, we've never met," Staff A added quickly, shouting over from his position in the front seat. "Now make sure you all do up your seatbelts."

"She clicked hers around her and sort smiled at me, putting out a delicate hand for me to shake. I was struggling to get the seat belt done up, it simply wouldn't go around me so I abandoned it and put my hand out to shake hers. In horror, I realised that my hand was about four times the size of hers. Her tiny, delicate little pink nails looked like those of a child next to my hands which look like shovels.

God, life was so depressing. I think my hands were bigger than hers when I was born. Hands and feet are things that are not supposed to be big if you're a woman.

At times like these, I long to be delicate, small and adorable. Or, if the truth be known, I'd settle for being more attractive than my mother. That shouldn't be too much for a woman to ask for, should it?

The journey to the villas we were staying in for the retreat took around an hour and a half in boiling sunshine. There was air-conditioning in the vehicle, but it was certainly nothing like strong enough to prevent us all feeling weak with the heat.

"Is there any chance you could turn the air-conditioning up a bit?" I asked.

"You're going to have to get used to this heat lady, you're going to be exercising in this all day every day for the rest of the week," said Staff A.

God how I wanted to punch him.

"She's right though, it is terribly hot, is there anything you can do?" said Yvonne.

"Let me have a look," he said. He fiddled with the dials at the front, and when he couldn't make the air-conditioning any colder, he handed her his notebook and advised her to fan herself. I looked from him to her and back again, and felt like the most unimportant, ugly person on Earth.

We arrived at the health camp (I shall insist on calling it that, even though it's a 'military fitness camp') after baking in the minivan and stepped out onto a street of pretty chalk-coloured houses. In the middle of the row of attractive homes in yellow, soft blue and pink, were four red brick houses. "There are Villa 1, Villa 2, Villa 3 and Villa 4," said Staff B. "You are all in Villa 3. Please note that all food is served in Villa 1 and all classes and walks start from Villa 1. That is the main base of the activities. You are all free to go into any of the villas, but your bedrooms are in Villa 1. The keys to each of the villas are kept under the large stones outside the front doors. Once you've let yourself in, please replace the key so that the next person can also let themselves in. If you accidentally take the key with you, you'll cause chaos. Also, the bedrooms don't lock, so you won't need a lock for them. You'll find it's quite safe. Understand?"

We all nodded to indicate our understanding, but it wasn't enough for grumpy Staff A.

"What was that?" he asked, turning around.

We all murmured that yes, that was fine.

"When you're asked a question, you respond with 'yes staff'. OK?"

"Yes staff," we all said.

"And you understand that you mustn't move the key from under the rock?"

"Yes staff," we all said.

"OK then, let's go."

It was a beautiful place, very quiet and with these lovely bright orange and red flowers popping out all over the place - in baskets outside the villa and even from between the cracks in the wall.

"Come to Villa 1 at 5pm," said Staff B. "We'll run through the programme for the rest of the week and then go for a quick walk before dinner. OK?"

"Yes, staff," we all replied, as I bounced my case and mum's bag down the old stone steps towards the front door of the villa. I noticed that Yvonne had gone off with Staff A and Staff B. Definitely something fishy going on there.

CHAPTER FIVE: WALKING AND FAINTING

After the drama of the soldiers frog marching us to the minibus and the shock of discovering that my mother is way more fanciable than I am, it was a relief to open the door to the villa and discover that it was gorgeous inside...really lovely. There was a central seating area with three large sofas around a television, a large balcony with a table and chairs on it, and a good-sized kitchen complete with washing machine.

The room that mum and I were sharing was downstairs, so I lugged the two bags down the 12 steps and pushed open the door to the room.

When I looked inside, I gasped with relief. I was half expecting bunk beds and camouflage-patterned duvet covers with khaki towels, and no running water, but it was like a lovely hotel room. The best thing was the floor to ceiling glass doors that swept open onto a patio, with a swimming pool beyond.

"Oh my," said mum. "This looks lovely."

We dumped our bags on the beds and opened the patio

doors before walking out to the pool where Simon and Graham were standing, staring into the water.

Karen walked over to join us. She had very short dark hair that was cut like a man's hair, and quite big features. She wasn't unattractive, just not 'pretty' much to my relief.

"Thank God!" she said as she arrived next to us. "I was worried that the rooms were going to be set up like a military dorm after seeing those two nutters who picked us up from the airport."

"Me too," I squealed, rather louder than I meant to. I was just so excited that the room was a proper hotel room and not a terrible army base. I was also pleased that she seemed as disconcerted by the army stuff as I was. I didn't want to be the only person on the camp who didn't know it was run by the army.

"I don't think I was made for soldiering," she said. "I'm just not good at being shouted at."

"Gosh, me neither," I said. "I hate it when people should at me. And look at the size of this arse - I was not built for running around all over the place."

Karen smiled and laughed, and in that moment an unlikely bond was created between Karen and me, a bond built on mutual dislike of khaki and mud and a solidarity to avoid all military-related activity at all costs.

She high fived me and I smiled warmly. I'd made a friend. Not the sort of friend who'd be with me for a lifetime, but someone who'd help keep me sane over the coming days.

The only downside of chatting away to Karen was that I had left mum at the mercy of Simon. I looked round as she giggled girlishly. Simon looked away as I gave him the death stare that I normally save for customers in the DIY centre who move all the plants to the wrong places.

Simon scurried off and mum came to join me as we sat on the recliners, next to the pool and soaked up the remainder of the afternoon's sunshine. It was heaven...blue skies, a glistening pool and a couple of hours in which to relax.

We'd been told to meet in villa number one at 5pm and it was 3pm now. From there we would all go for a walk before dinner. It all seemed reassuringly civilised. I had a nice room, I'd made a nice friend and now I was going on a walk before dinner. Perhaps this whole thing would be OK after all?

I drifted off to sleep until mum woke me up at quarter to five. As soon as I opened my eyes I was absolutely starving. The sun was still beating down on me. I needed a very large gin and tonic and a very large burger and fries.

"Are we eating before going on the walk?" I asked.

"I don't think so," she replied. She'd changed into the gym gear that we bought in Sports Direct and looked like she was about to race in the Olympic 100m event.

I staggered out of the sunshine and into the cool haven of my room. I hadn't unpacked and really couldn't be bothered to.

"Do you think I'll be OK in these sandals?" I asked mum. "I can't be bothered to unpack my whole case to get my trainers out."

"Well, obviously trainers would be better," she responded, "but it's only a light evening walk so I'm sure you'll be fine in those on the first night."

So we headed upstairs in the villa, then strode up the stone steps onto the main road and headed down to villa one.

The main villa was very similar in layout to ours, but a little bit bigger, and a bit more bedraggled, if the truth be known. Perhaps it was the fact that so many people sat on the sofas in that villa because it was where everyone congregated meaning everything looked more worn and tired. In our villa we had lovely, plump cream sofas, whereas here they were bedraggled orange ones, with a range of mismatching scatter cushions. I much preferred our villa. Mum and I hovered on the edge of the main room, peering in, unsure whether we should just enter.

"Come in, come in," said a very thin, very fit looking woman, emerging from a side room: you must be from the Two Fat Ladies blog? I'm Abigail."

"Yes, I'm from Two Fat Ladies. I'm Mary," I said. "This is my mum."

"Hello there, nice to meet you," she said. "I really hope you enjoy yourself over the next few days. I'm sure you'll get a lot out of it." Then she glanced at mum: "You're not fat at all. You look great," she said.

"Thank you, how kind," said mum, blushing.

I know Abi's right, mum does look great, but it still felt like a dagger through me that I was absolutely as fat as she expected but mum wasn't. I know I look fat, but I still find it very hard when I realise that other people see me as fat, or when I'm made to feel fat.

After the pleasantries (or 'unpleasantries' in my case), we all went for what they laughing called an evening stroll. Trades Descriptions Act anyone? My idea of an evening stroll is a gentle, enjoyable walk at a sensible pace.

Their idea of an evening stroll is trying to break some sort of imaginary world record even if it means killing everyone in the group. I tried to keep up, I really did, but the combined forces of strappy sandals, gross unfitness and a body which is twice as large as it should be, prevented me from finishing anywhere near the others. I was about 20 minutes behind them. It was ridiculous, absolutely ridiculous.

"Come on," mum said, in the end, "I could have done the walk five times while you've done it once."

"OK, OK," I said. "Just relax. It's day one, no point in wearing yourself out when we've only just started. I'm saving myself for later in the week."

The simple truth, of course, was that I was going as fast as I possibly could, and it was the fastest they were likely to see me all week, if - indeed - I could tolerate staying all week.

By the time I got back to the villa I felt more exhausted than I ever have in my life before. I was also completely starving and really thirsty.

"Water?" said Staff B, handing me a beaker. I just nodded at him. I'd completely lost the power of speech.

I was aware that I would be absolutely scarlet and soaking wet with sweat - I always was after exercise, but this time I felt much worse than I usually do. I could feel my head spinning, and kept staggering as I stood there. My knees buckled a bit but I managed to gain my composure. I'd be fine in a minute. I sipped on the water, and waited to feel whole again.

"Are you sure you're OK?" asked mum. "You really don't look very well."

"Of course I am," I said, once my voice had come back and I'd stopped shaking.

"You're absolutely bright red you know."

"Yes, I do that when I'm tired," I said. "I'm feeling much better now."

As I spoke, I felt everything spin. I felt all unsteady. I heard mum's shout but it all sounded so far away, I remembered grabbing hold of something that fell to the ground, making a massive sound, and I remember trying to apologise as I hit the deck, then I don't really remember anything else.

CHAPTER SIX: AN INCIDENT WITH DONALD

"She's moving.... she's opening her eyes..."

I could hear mum's voice floating above me,

"Can you hear me love?" she was saying. "Clap if you can hear me."

I moved my hands in a clapping motion and made the tiniest sound - the most pathetic sound in the history of clapping. There was a great cheer and everyone in the room started clapping too. I looked up to see them all looking down at me, applauding my attempt at a clap, their faces full of pride at my achievement. I felt like a toddler who'd just used the potty for the first time.

"Are you feeling alright," said a familiar voice.

"Um, yes, I think," I said vaguely. "Is that you, mum?"

"Yes, darling, it's me," she said.

"Where am I?" I couldn't work out where on earth I was. The people looking down at me looked familiar, but they weren't my friends. Who were they? Why were they here, in my bedroom?

"You're at the weight loss camp, remember?" said mum.

"We went for a long walk earlier and you couldn't keep up, then you came back and just fell to the ground."

"Oh God, yes. The weight loss camp. Oh God. I wish I hadn't asked."

"We're all about to have supper. Perhaps it'll help you if we get some food inside you...what do you think?" said a male voice, before Staff B's face loomed into view. He smiled at me, and given his position above me, looking down at me, all I could think of was sex. He looked particularly gorgeous from that angle. I knew I needed to move before I pulled him down on top of me and started dry humping him.

"Food sounds like a good idea," I said, sitting up and looking at the faces around me. They all looked so concerned.

"Come and sit down," said Karen. "See if you feel better after dinner."

I was helped to my feet by the two 'staffs' and led to the end of the wooden table. The others came over to join me.

"Sit here," Staff B said, pulling out a wooden chair with his gloved hand (still wearing gloves? Very odd) and seating me.

"I'll bring out the food now. Does everyone else want to sit down as well," said Abigail, wiggling her way into the kitchen, giving us all a sight of her peachy derriere clad in expensive lycra.

I continued to sip the beaker of water, and smiled as a bowl was laid before me. I peered inside it and looked at mum. She was nodding at me with a look of victory on her face. The bowl contained orange liquid. She was right. We'd been here just a few hours and already they were serving us bloody carrots.

Dinner didn't take too long, as you can probably imagine. Boiled, mashed carrots don't demand a lot of chewing. I finished and waited patiently for something else...anything else - even a celery stick or an apple would have been nice - you know - something to chew on, get my teeth into. But that was it. Just a bowl full of carroty baby food.

"That was actually quite filling, wasn't it?" said Yvonne, helping me to my feet and asking whether I was OK.

She led me over to the orange sofas and sat me down gently. Everyone else had sat down too. There were about 20 of us on the course, five in each villa. There were people of all shapes and sizes, but none as shapely as me. They all seemed very kind and genuinely concerned about me, which was nice, even Simon the mother-stalker handed me a cushion and asked whether I needed anything.

I sat back into the sofa and felt quite relaxed. It had been a dramatic start to the trip, but the people were all nice, the accommodation was lovely and if I ate like that, I'd lose about 40 stone by the end of the week, so it wasn't all bad.

"Shall we play a game," said a guy with ginger hair and a rather unflattering ginger goatee beard. I didn't know the guy at all. I knew his name was Mark because he'd introduced himself to me on the walk earlier, but he wasn't in our villa so I knew nothing about him. I liked him though. He had been kind enough to offer to stay back and keep me company on the walk earlier while the others had stormed ahead like they were heading into battle.

"Yes, a game sounds good," I replied, more because I thought he was a nice guy so wanted to support him than because I have any interest at all in playing games.

"Yes," said another guy I didn't know. "If there's no eating or drinking allowed this evening, a game would be a good distraction."

"OK," said Mark. "I'm going to pose a question then we have to go around the room and all answer it. It'll help us to get to know one another as well. Make sure you say your name before you answer."

I was slightly concerned about this - not for my sake - I'm quite outgoing and happy to answer any questions, but mum's so reserved - I knew she wouldn't want to answer any personal questions.

"What's the weirdest memory you have of school?" asked Mark.

Fast as lightning mum's hand shot up.

"I remember a teacher at school being sacked once," she said, laughing as she spoke. "It was so strange…there was an eagle's nest outside and all the children had to go and look at it on Fridays. For some reason it always fell to this particular teacher to take us and she got completely fed up, so one afternoon, when she thought everyone had left the building, she picked up some rocks and hurled them at the nest. It was alarming. I think they were endangered at the time. The birds squawked, the caretaker came and Mrs Thatchmaker was escorted from the building. No one saw her again, nor the eagles. I don't know whether she killed them or terrified them so much that the mummy eagle decided to move them somewhere safer."

I was flabbergasted. Where had mum suddenly got all this confidence from?

"That's so funny. You're a gifted storyteller," said Simon, smiling at mum until he saw me watching him closely and turned away. I swear, if I haven't strangled him by the end of this holiday it will be a bloody miracle.

"How about you, Simon? Do you have a story from your school days?" I asked, hoping to catch him out without a tale to tell.

"Well, I have a rather vivid and disconcerting memory that I could share with you," he said.

"Do go on," said Yvonne.

"In junior school our English teacher would put on a new coat of lipstick in in the brightest red colour, and kiss the boys whenever they misbehaved in class," he said. "Once she'd kissed one of us, we weren't allowed to wipe it off. It happened to me and it was mortifying...I never crossed her again."

"That's rather a good idea," said mum. "Disciplining the boys without resorting to violence. I like that. I might adopt that if anyone crosses me. I'll kiss them on the cheek and that will stop them."

"Now I really want to cross you," said Simon, smiling lasciviously at mum, causing everyone in the room to look slightly awkward.

"Right, on that note, I'm going to head off to bed. Are you coming, mum?"

"Oh. Actually, I thought I might stay here for a little while and play this game," she said. "Why don't you stay and join in?"

"I just need to get some sleep," I said, though - in truth - I had a little snack secreted in my bag, and I needed to eat it before I died of hunger.

"I'll come and walk you back," said mum.

"No, no - you stay. I'll be fine. It takes about 10 seconds to get back. I'll see you later."

"See you in the morning," said Karen, offering a friendly wave.

"I'll walk out with you - I'm heading out," said Yvonne, leaning over to help me to my feet.

"Where are you going?" I asked, hoping upon hope that she was heading out to the pub. If she was going to a pub, I was definitely going with her. I really needed a drink; I wanted to do an 'Aunty Susan', and drink and eat my way through the evening.

"I've found a lovely hotel on the seafront with a great gym with a sauna and spa. I'm going to do a quick work out and sit in the sauna before bed."

"Really?" I said. It baffled me that anyone would want to do extra exercise. "Don't overdo it though - we've got loads on tomorrow without you trying to squeeze in any extra voluntary stuff tonight."

"I won't overdo it" she said. "See you later."

She walked away in shorts so tight they must have been stitched on by her gynaecologist.

I loitered near the door for a minute, listening to mum and the others still telling their stories. "Come on, a few more silly tales," mum was saying. "I'm enjoying this. Actually, I remember something my husband told me. It's a very funny story; he was in his science class and the teacher was introducing them to the subject of electricity. The teacher told the whole class to hold hands, with the children on the end holding a generator. He was going to give them a little tingle of electricity and demonstrate how humans conducted it as it went all along the line of children. But the teacher had it turned up way too high and he electrocuted half of them. Your father was in hospital for a week and had terrible burns on his hands."

"Oh, my goodness," said Staff B, joining the group. "Did that happen to you?"

"No, my husband," said mum.

He looked over at me. "How are you feeling now?"

"OK," I said. "I was just leaving. I feel really tired."

"You should get an early night. If you're not feeling right tomorrow, I'll call a doctor and we'll get him to take a look at you."

"OK," I said. "I'm sure I'll be fine, I just over did it."

"All the more reason to get an early night then," said Staff B. "Do you want me to walk with you?"

"No, I'll be fine," I said. "Karen, would you mind making sure mum gets back safely?"

"Of course," she said. "No problem at all."

"Thank you. Good night everyone," I said, heading through

the door as they resumed their game and told silly stories about their time at school. It was only a few steps back to the villa - I walked up the stone steps, through the gate, along to the next villa, down the steps and took the key from under the stone, I let myself in and walked down to the bedroom. It had seemed odd that the rooms didn't lock when I first arrived, but now it was a Godsend - I just pushed the door open, wandered inside and slumped onto the bed. I couldn't be bothered to unpack my suitcase and find my nightie, so I just stripped off, dumped my phone on the bedside cabinet and climbed between the sheets. I fell fast asleep as soon as my head touched the pillow.

And, to be fair, that's exactly where I would have stayed had it not been for the feel of someone getting into the bed next to me and jumping back out again.

"Who the hell are you?" said a male voice.

I hastily pushed the light on and there stood a man in his 60s in his Y-fronts. I recognised him from earlier but didn't know his name. I certainly hadn't invited him to join me.

"Get out of my room," I screamed, wrapping the duvet around me as I sat up. "Get out."

"This is my room," said the man.

"This is not your room. It's my room. I share it with my mum."

"Look around," he said. "I've got all my stuff here…see…. You're very welcome to stay, but it's not your room."

He was right. His things were laid out on the dressing table, his trainers were neatly by the long mirror. There was no sign of my unpacked suitcase anywhere. Nor any sign of mum.

"Oh shit," I said, wrapping his sheet around me and gathering my clothes together. "I don't know how this happened."

"This is villa two," he said. He was staring at my body, not looking at my face while I spoke to him.

"Oh God, I'm villa three," I said. "I'll be off now."

"No, stay," he said. "Why don't you stay here. I can look after you. I'm Donald, by the way."

"Err, no thanks. I'm going," I said, and I ran from the room, ran up the stairs and into the right room in the right villa. Thankfully mum wasn't back yet, so I climbed into the right bed and fell asleep.

Jesus Christ, Mary, great start to the trip.

CHAPTER SEVEN: SWING YOUR ARMS, MARY

The alarm clock burst into life at 5.30am and mum leapt out of bed like a wild salmon. "Come on, up you get," she said. "Remember we've got our walk this morning before breakfast."

"A walk? You're joking, right? Were you not there for that walk last night? It was a travesty. We must've done about 20 miles. It almost killed me. Perhaps I shouldn't come this morning?"

"Gosh you do exaggerate, you'll be fine, just remember to wear your trainers and drink lots of water," said mum pulling back the floor-to-ceiling curtains and letting a most unwelcome flash of early morning light into the room. The pool in the courtyard was glittering in the morning sunshine, just outside the patio doors.

"Oh my God - I've just remembered something," I said, staring at the pool. "Last night...something really weird happened."

"What?" asked mum. "When I got in, you were fast asleep."

"Yes - before that. Oh God."

Mum was looking at me intently but I couldn't find the words to explain to her.

"What happened?" she asked, all wide-eyed, dressed in nothing but her sports bra and an offensively large pair of pants.

"I fainted," I said, "I just remembered that I fainted."

She didn't need to know that I'd jumped into the bed of a 60-year-old called Donald.

"Yes, you did," she said kindly. "Are you feeling OK now?"

"Much better," I said.

I clambered out of bed and started to look around for my phone. I couldn't see it anywhere. I got that horrible lurching feeling in the pit of my stomach that appeared whenever I couldn't find my phone.

"Shit."

I tipped out the contents of my handbag and wracked my brain.

"What on earth's the matter?" asked mum. "What have you lost?"

"My phone. I don't know what I've done with it."

"You probably left it in villa one last night. Let's check when we get there. Or maybe it fell out of your pocket when you fainted?"

"Yes, probably," I said. "Maybe I should look for my phone instead of the walk? I could catch up with you all later?"

"No, you're coming on the walk," said mum. "We've come all this way to get fit and healthy...this is a great chance for you to lose some weight and start to feel good. It's silly to start missing out on things on day one."

"OK, OK," I said. "I'll come on the walk, but you have to be aware that if it's anything like last night's walk, it will kill me and there's every chance that you'll be arrested for murder for making me go on it."

"The walk last night was about five miles, that's all, and it was very nice. All the people we met were lovely, and the scenery was spectacular. Come on, up you get. We're walking along the beach this morning, then hopefully we'll have time to come back and jump in that pool afterwards. Doesn't it look spectacular? Just spectacular."

"I knew it was a mistake bringing you," I said, as I staggered like a drunk into the bathroom. Why couldn't my mum be miserable in the mornings like everyone else on earth? As I clambered into the shower, I could hear her singing to herself as she got changed. God, the backs of my legs were aching. The truth was that I was so bloody unfit that every bit of exercise we did was going to render me feeling exhausted and in pain. Mum, on the other hand, was a regular walker, played a bit of tennis, and did a lot of gardening. In short, she was about 30 years older than me but twice as fit as me. And if that wasn't an embarrassing prospect, I thought to myself as I washed my hair and clambered out of the shower, I didn't know what was.

I followed mum out of the room, my hair was still wet and my unforgiving gym kit made me feel the size of a house. We walked to villa one where we were all meeting. I shuffled along in a sulk, staring at the ground while mum strode ahead, and shouted 'morning' to everyone she encountered. I decided I was not saying good morning to anyone.

"Mary, Mary," came a shout from a man running towards us. I gasped when I saw him. It was Donald - the guy from last night...the guy who had come into his room and seen me in fast-asleep in his bed. Oh God. In his hand he held my phone.

"You left this is my room," he said. I looked at him aghast, alarm spreading across my face like an uncontrollable rash. He mistook my alarm for confusion. "When you were in my bed last night. Remember? Well, you left this behind."

I looked at mum who was open-mouthed.

"It's not how it looks," I mouthed. "I went into his bed by mistake."

Mum's mouth was still wide open.

"IT WAS A MISTAKE."

"I'll say it was," she said. "Having an affair with an older man on holiday when you have such a lovely boyfriend at home...a huge mistake."

"Mum, I didn't have an affair. I went to the wrong villa, that's all. They all look the same, the doors aren't locked. It was an easy mistake to make."

Mum looked at me and shook her head.

"Do you really think I would cheat on Ted?" I said. "Ted is the nicest man in the world, I'd never do anything to upset him, you must know that."

"Of course I do. I'm just teasing you."

We both looked up and saw Staff B ahead, warning up by bending over in perilously tight shorts. "One word of advice though, Mary. If you do decide to get into a man's bed accidentally, get into the bed of a man like Staff B, not dopey Donald, won't you."

"Will do," I said as Staff B stood up. He had on the shortest shorts, but still wore a long-sleeved t-shirt and those white gloves he seemed obsessed with. He was stubbly and muscular and oozed masculinity. Mum was right. That would definitely have been a better bed to have found myself in.

"Ready for our little morning walk," he said, giving me a gentle hug. "You don't have to look so sad. It's only a quick stroll along the beach."

"I'm not sad," I said. "I just don't believe you. It won't be a quick walk at all: I'm wise to your madness now. I'm well aware that when you say a quick walk along the beach you mean that we're going to do an Ironman triathlon in world record beating time."

"Not quite," he said with a warm laugh. "It's just a morning stroll to knock away the cobwebs."

He grinned as he walked away but I knew he was lying. 'Stroll'? Really? I didn't think it would be at all stroll-ish.

I went and sat on the small stone wall outside the villa while everyone else warmed up. I knew I should join in, but I felt so self-conscious, so I sat and focused on the lovely purple flowers growing out of the rocks next to us, gently cupping one of them in my hand and making a mental note to find out what they were, they were so beautiful - like tiny pansies with lovely, open faces. I looked up to see Donald watching me and I felt myself blush as I looked away. How could I have been so bloody stupid?

Everyone else was ready to go, some of them jogging on the spot and waving their arms around, some starting to stretch their calves out like they were bloody Paula Radcliffe or something. Then it was time to leave...

We all walked down the street, quite fast. Much faster than I would've chosen to do had I been walking by myself, I had to do little skippy steps to keep up with them. We then went down along the line of steps which led to the beach. "Come on, let's get a bit of speed up shall we," said Staff B, jogging down them, then sprinting out across the sand. Oh Christ. I just wasn't fit enough to do any of this, as I ran down the steps, I could feel my boobs bouncing up and down and my stomach moving like it had a mind of its own. Instinctively I pulled my t-shirt down and held it flat against my body as if to disguise the horrible flesh beneath it. I hated being fat. Being fat was horrible.

"What's up with you?" said Staff B. "You look like you're really fed up. Look at your mum, she's out there jogging along the beach."

"You said it would be a walk," I bit back.

I looked up to see mum running along with the others.

They were lifting their knees up as high as they could and had their arms out in front of them so that their knees were tapping against their hands. They were already miles in front.

"I can't do any of this because I'm too fat," I said, disconsolately. "It hurts when I run and skip and jump."

"Well, just walk then. The important thing is to keep moving."

"I'm not going to lose all this weight by walking, am I?" I said.

"Yes, of course you will. If you vow to move whenever you can, however you want, you'll lose the weight. It's not rocket science."

"But it will take years of effort and I haven't got the motivation for it."

"You don't need motivation. Stop thinking of exercising as some sort of horrible punishment. Look, this is how I see it. First thing - speed up a little bit and walk next to me. That's not too bad, is it? Walking at this speed where you can feel yourself getting out of breath will use a lot more calories."

"OK, I can do that," I said.

"Now, swing your arms as you walk," he said. I swung them by my side. "See how fast you can swing them," he said. I swung them backwards and forwards as quickly as I could and noticed that my pace was speeding up.

"A little tip for you there, Mary," he said. "You will find that your legs will go as fast as your arms are swinging, so if you want to make yourself go faster just swing your arms faster and your legs will keep up. If you walk along like you have been doing with your arms hardly swinging at all, you will find that you automatically walk more slowly."

"Good tip," I said.

"And you know what you've just been saying to me about losing weight?"

"Yes," I said, hoping he was going to give me some magical

formula for losing weight that would enable me to shift 10 stone this week.

"I think you need to stop thinking about it as being all about weight loss. Yes, you want to lose weight, but you want weight loss to be the by-product of what you do to get yourself feeling fit healthy and wonderful.

"I think the what you need to focus on is looking after yourself a bit more. So, don't put anything in your mouth that isn't going to do you good. Drink lots of water because it will stop you having headaches and make you feel full of energy, and just use your legs and your body as much as you can because being fit is the key to feeling great.

"All you are doing from now onwards is looking after yourself and trying to feel as great and wonderful as possible.

"Stop trying to tick off the number of pounds you've lost, and stop mentally totting up how many months it's going to be before you meet some arbitrary desired weight. Just take each day as it comes and, on that day, do everything you can to make yourself feel and look better. How about that as a plan?"

The arm swinging seemed to be working well, and I had almost caught up with the rest of the group who were busy doing star jumps on the side of the beach near the cliff.

"Okay, I can do that," I said. "Thank you."

He leaned in and gave me a big hug and said: "You know, Mary Brown, it's all going to be okay. You're young, attractive, and prepared to do something to make yourself fitter and healthier. You've got a lovely life ahead of you - you've just got to believe that."

"I believe," I said in a loud, mock American accent, being sarcastic with him as he smiled and walked away, but the truth was that I did feel quite good, better than I had for ages, and I did feel as if I believed I could do something about the way I looked. I smiled at his retreating back and thought. "This could be the best week of my life."

Then I saw Donald approaching, clutching a small purple flower like the ones I'd been admiring earlier. "Hello bed mate," he said, with an unattractive wink. "Thought you might like this…"

CHAPTER EIGHT: WEIGHTS AND MEASURES

"Right, let's get going on with the weighing and measuring," said Staff A, clapping his hands and rubbing them together. "We want to make sure that you know exactly where you are beginning of the course so you can see how much you progress in just a few days."

This struck me as odd. Hadn't Staff B just spent 10 minutes having an emotional chat with me on the beach in which he said that I shouldn't focus on weight?"

I couldn't resist mentioning this…in the hope that they would abandon their plans to weigh us.

"Yes, Mary, that's true," he said, a hint of exasperation sneaking into the corners of his voice. "But this is to help you see what impact we can have when we work really hard. It's a motivational tool more than anything else. Does that make sense?"

"Yes," I said. Though it didn't really. I didn't understand why a course which decried the process of weighing and measuring, weighed and measured us all at the beginning and the end of the course.

I think he could sense that I was still very confused. "OK, I can see that it seems odd," he said. "I wouldn't advise worrying too much about your weight, look at how you look and how you feel and what makes you happy rather than what random numbers on a scale tell you.

"We are all different builds, all different makeups, the idea that everybody who is 5'6" should weigh the same is simply wrong, but it's a useful guide to see how you've changed over the course."

I nodded at him, realising that I wasn't going to get out of this and they were going to measure me regardless. I suppose the weighing gives them a handy marketing tool: 'lose half a stone in four days' is a lot more exciting a proposition than 'get a bit healthier, but not measurably so because we don't believe in measuring and weighing.'

I was first up. That would teach me to answer back to the instructor. I stepped onto the scales and watched the numbers in front of me rising with astounding speed, getting bigger and bigger until they settled on… 20 stone and 4 pounds.

"That's wrong!" I squealed, jumping off as if the thing had bitten me. I saw the looks of horror on the faces of those waiting in the dining room for their turn to be measured. A bit like that time I screamed in the dentists at such blood-curdling volume that the waiting room had cleared by the time I came out.

"I can't possibly be that heavy. That's the weight a baby elephant should be, or a car or something, not a human being."

"Don't worry about it," said Staff A with a smile. "It's just a number. It just tells you where you are now, and then we can see where you are at the end of the week, and work out what changes have taken place."

"But to be over 20 stone…that's insane," I said. "Your scales are drunk."

"Twenty stone!" squealed mum. "That can't be right can it?"

"No!" I shouted back. "It most certainly isn't."

"You told me you were 15 stone."

"I am," I said. "The scales are wrong."

I looked at Staff A. "The scales are right, aren't they?" I said miserably.

"Yep," he said. "But try not to worry. You're in the right place with the right people I will help you sort all this out. OK?"

"Yes," I said.

I walked back to mum.

"That can't be right," she said.

"No," I said, shaking my head vigorously.

"So, the scales were wrong?" she asked.

"Yes," I said. "They hadn't set them up properly."

"So, how heavy are you?" asked mum.

"Fifteen stone," I replied.

Mum went on next and came skipping back to declare that she was 10 and half stone. "I'm really pleased because I thought my weight was creeping up towards 11 stone."

"Yes, that would have been awful," I said, uncharitably, while I chewed on the fact that mum was about half my weight.

It took a little while for the whole weighing process to happen, so we were treated to a film to keep us entertained while they did it. Not a film in the way you or I might recognise it - no Sex & The City or Bridesmaids or anything, just a film about being healthy and getting fit. And no popcorn, of course. Not even the naff plain stuff that I accidentally buy sometimes by mistake when I'm aiming for the toffee coated stuff.

Staff B stepped up to sort out the video, and after a considerable amount of trouble connecting his laptop to the large screen, including him showing everyone all his emails, he appeared to have asserted some sort of technological control.

"Phew," he said. "That was harder than I thought it would

be. OK. Before we start on today's sessions, and while the weighing is going on, we have a quick video to show you. Before I do that, a quick question - who was alarmed by their weight and is disappointed at weighing more than they thought they would?"

Loads of hands shot up, including bone-skinny Yvonne's which really annoyed me. I bet her weight hardly registered on the scale.

"Well, I want you to stop worrying - the reason for us weighing you is just to show you that if you eat right and exercise well, you WILL lose weight. But we'd very much like you to park the whole weight issue.

"As staff explained to Mary earlier, we mustn't put too much emphasis on how much we weigh. What's important is how you feel, and to most of you it'll be how you look. I'm sure you'd much rather look great in a dress than hit a particular weight measurement but not look great. Isn't that right?"

"Yes," we all chorused.

"And how are you all feeling today?"

"Fat!" I shouted, while everyone else shouted "great."

The video shimmered into life and a rather sombre-looking guy, dressed in a white coat like a doctor or scientist, appeared on the screen.

"Obesity is such a problem that we spend more on it than on the fire service, the police service and the judiciary all put together," he said.

Sighs of disbelief drifted in from all corners of the room.

"It's alarming isn't it?" he continued. "It shows what a problem it is. And it also shows how hard it is to deal with - do you know why that is? Why don't we all just eat less?

"The reason is in our biology - it's because we are forcing ourselves to live a life that suits our minds, not our bodies. We have bodies that are designed to store food and a brain that is designed to be attracted to food - these are survival instincts that worked when food was scarce. But now we're living in a part of the world where there's plenty of food while these instincts remain.

"So - what you're all wondering is - what do we do about it? These facts might help to give you a clue: we are now 20% less active than we were back in the 1960s. Exercise is a vital part of good health."

There were mumblings of agreement and I mumbled along with them but to be honest, I don't think exercise is the key to anything but abject misery.

"Exercise is one of five things you need to do to lose weight. Numerous investigations have shown this. These are the five things: eat less, exercise more, drink water when you're hungry, remember that your body was designed for times when there was no food around and it had to carefully conserve everything you put into it, and – finally - walk, walk and walk again."

I was starting to get really frustrated with the whole thing. If I could 'eat less' I wouldn't be obese in the first place.

"There are lots of diets being promoted all the time," science man was continuing. "Lots of them marketed as the answer to all your weight loss problems. But there are real issues associated with opting for the latest fad diet, or the diet that appears to be 'proven' to be the best way to lose weight. Let me demonstrate."

Suddenly science man was standing in front of a university.

"So, a study, conducted at this university, found that low-carb dieters fared much better than those who followed a low-fat diet and showed better results on blood tests that indicate cardiovascular health.

"Then a few months later, a University of South Carolina

study published in the International Journal of Applied and Basic Nutritional Sciences found the greatest weight loss was found on a high-carbohydrate vegan diet.

So, within two months, the evidence points to the fact that low-carb diets work, and high-carb diets work.

"There have been reports that depression and obesity are strongly linked, that eating breakfast helps you lose weight, and then, a few months later, further research to show that none of that is true.

"The reason I'm saying all this is to show you that having a healthy scepticism about studies is important. Some are good, some are bad. Even the good ones can be overturned with another study a few years on."

The video ended with a montage of good old-fashioned advice about eating a healthy, balanced diet: Don't eat too much, drink lots of water and avoid mood-altering foods like sugar-laden drinks, cakes and coffee that send your hormones into overdrive."

"So, what do you all think of that?" said Staff B.

No one spoke, so I thought I ought to.

"Oh God. It's all so complicated," I said.

"Exactly. The point is that if you try to do fad diet plans or exercise regimes, or try to miss out one food group in an effort to shed the pounds, you are unlikely to achieve a good result long term. If you keep it simple and follow our advice - not only will you look better, but you'll all be much healthier. Does that make sense?"

"Yes," I said. It did make sense. I was sick of following stupid diet fads. I would give this a go."

"Good. So, on that note, let me introduce you to today's activities."

He pulled out a blackboard that was full of classes. I swear to God, there were 10 on there.

"Are you having a laugh?" I asked, more loudly than I intended to.

"You don't have to do all the classes," said Staff A, but you'll get a much better result if you do everything."

"The result will be me in intensive care," I said.

"No one wants that," said the instructor. "Just do whatever you can and try to push yourself as much as possible."

I sensed that my constant talking back at him was starting to wear a bit thin. Still, the blackboard. You should have bloody seen it: First was boxing, then circuits, then cycling, followed by swimming and that was all before lunch. In the afternoon something called heat, followed by body combat, body conditioning, body pump and Pilates, then more boxing. JESUS CHRIST

"Before all that, though - breakfast," he said.

Possibly the only sensible thing anyone has said since I arrived in this God-forsaken place.

CHAPTER NINE: STAFF B COMES TO VISIT

The day was exhausting. I mean - terrifyingly tiring, and I only did half of it. I opted for missing out every other class so that I could cope with it all. The day was to end with a final boxing class held on the top of a steep hill, which practically took crampons and advanced mountaineering equipment to climb. I sat on the edge of my bed. Would it really be so bad if I didn't go? I'd missed the first boxing class in the morning, but in my defence, I had been to more classes that day than I'd been to in the previous year, and there were two more days to go. Surely I could miss this one out?

Under the pretence of looking for my water bottle, I told mum to go on ahead and I'd join her.

"OK," she said, smiling and dancing out of the room. Honestly, she's indefatigable.

As soon as she had gone, I flopped onto the bed and experienced a moment of utter joy and exhilaration, lying there, eyes closed, with the sun warming me through the patio windows. Without moving from my position on the bed I eased off my trainers, pushing down the back of the heel with my other foot, and hearing the gentle plop as it hit the floor. I did the same with the other trainer and lay back about as comfortable as any woman has ever been in her life before.

As I felt myself slinking into the bed, and dropping off to sleep, I heard a gentle knock at the door. It must be mum. She must've realised that I wasn't coming and had come back for me. "I'm too tired for boxing," I shouted. "I'm going to have a little sleep before dinner."

It wasn't mum's voice that replied but a deep male voice. "Can I come in? It's Staff B."

I sat up in the bed, ran my hands through my hair and adjusted my clothing to look as alluring as possible. Well, as alluring as a 20 and a half stone woman can look in lycra when she's been exercising all day. I cursed myself for not having come in and had a shower.

"Of course," I said. I arranged myself as seductively as possible, my head resting against my hand, my arm bent, one leg over the other as I lay on my side, in the hope that I would look feminine and elegant.

"Hello there," he said, walking inside and taking a seat in the chair next to my bed. "Everything okay?"

"Yes, fine," I said. "I just feel completely knackered. I couldn't face boxing. I'm also weak with hunger. I just don't cope very well without food."

"Well that's what I wanted to talk to you about," said Staff B. "You didn't come along for the snack just now before boxing. Everyone else was desperate for it. I figured perhaps you weren't feeling very well?"

"Snack?" I said. "I didn't know there was a snack?"

"Yes." That's when he presented me with a tiny piece of flapjack. Honestly it was minuscule... about the size of my thumbnail, but nothing has ever given me greater pleasure.

"Is this for me?" I asked, as if he just given me a jumbo jet or something.

"All yours," he said. I picked it up off the plate as if it was the most precious thing ever, and put it onto the end of my tongue, determined to make it last as long as possible

"I can't believe I missed a snack," I said to Staff B. "I've never missed a snack in my life before."

He smiled warmly.

"Why aren't you with the boxers?" I asked.

"We're mixing things up - Staff A and Abi are taking this one so I can get a couple of hours off. I've got a bit of paperwork to do, and I'm working the session tomorrow as well as being in charge of the great big martial arts, combat and boxing three-hour marathon session on Thursday morning."

"WHAT?"

"Yep - three hours of boxing, kicking and wrestling. Pure joy"

"Good God this is hardcore," I said. "Why so much boxing and fighting?"

"It's a military fitness camp. What did you think we'd be doing? Needlework?"

"Ha, ha," I said. "Can I ask you something?"

"Fire away," he said.

"Why are you called Staff B? It seems really weird that we can't just call you by your name."

"My name is Martin," he said. "But here they like the instructors to be called staff."

"Why? It's absurd, to insist on everything being so military when we're just a bunch of flabby people wanting to lose a few pounds."

"Yes," he said, with a smile. "But there is a sensible reason. You see – in the army when you're a PT instructor you don't have a rank, you're all called staff, so no one knows what rank you are. The reason for that is that physical fitness is very important, and you couldn't have a situation where the physical trainer is instructing someone of a higher rank, and the person of the higher rank didn't want to do it so pulled rank.

"They decided the best thing was that when it came to physical training everyone involved was just called staff and were all equal."

"Oh, I see, "I said. "That makes sense. I can see why they would do that. Why on earth don't they explain that to us, it would make us all feel much better about the names we have to call you."

"I don't know really," said Staff B. "Maybe I'll mention it to Abi?"

"Did you like it in the army?" I asked.

"I loved it," he said, taking off his boots, putting his feet up on the bed and removing his watch as he made himself comfortable. Interestingly, the gloves stayed on.

"My dad was a soldier and my grandad before him. All of the men in my family end up in the army, it's in the blood. It's all I ever wanted to do, and when I got in the army, I felt like I'd come home. Then there was the tour to Afghanistan where it all went horribly wrong."

"What happened?"

"In short, I had my arm blown off," he said bluntly. "It's why I always wear long-sleeved shirts. Look…" He lifted his shirt sleeve and I could see the prosthetic arm beneath it. I'd never noticed before. He always wore gloves and always wore long sleeves, and no one was anyone the wiser.

"Gosh. Did someone shoot at you? What happened?"

"No, it was a landmine. It was in an area where we knew there were landmines, but I was much further out than we thought they went. Four of us were standing there. One guy died."

"Oh God. I'm so sorry," I said. "How awful"

"Yep," he said, nodding. "All pretty awful. When I left, I had no idea what I'd do with myself. Like I explained - being a soldier was in my blood...I couldn't think how I'd survive without it. Doing military-style training for civilians saved me. I couldn't have gone into an office job or anything, it would have driven me nuts. Or worked in a shop. Can you imagine that? Working in a shop all day…"

"I work in a shop," I said timidly.

"Oh. Sorry," he replied. "I just think it would have driven me insane."

"Don't worry. It drives me insane sometimes," I said. "What about Staff A? Was it the same sort of thing with him? Injured abroad."

Staff B moved to stand up. "No, it was very different with him. I better head off. I'll see you at dinner." With that he was gone, he had deliberately refused to talk about why Staff A had left the army. I knew, instinctively, that there was something odd about this. Staff B's reaction had triggered a little spark of interest in me. Right. That would be my mission. To find out why the guy had left the army and why he had such a close relationship with skinny Yvonne.

It wasn't long before mum came back from boxing looking so bedraggled and exhausted that I was doubly pleased I hadn't gone on the trip up the hill. "What happened to you?" she said, falling onto her bed like a rag doll. "You missed the snack and everything."

"Yes, sorry," I said.

"What's this?" Mum held up Staff B's watch, that he'd left on the edge of her bed.

"Oh yes - that's Staff B's," I said, not quite realising how dodgy that sounded.

She handed me the watch, her eyebrows raised so high they had disappeared into her hairline. "Staff B's," she said. "You know I wasn't serious when I said you should try to bed him next time. You know I was only joking, don't you?"

"Ha ha ha," I said. "You're so funny, mum. Nothing happened. He just came to see me."

"And undressed?"

"No, he didn't undress. He just took his watch off."

"Yep - very likely story," said mum. "Very likely story indeed."

"He dropped my snack off, if you must know. And he wanted to see how I was. I guess he thought it was so unlikely that I would miss the chance of food that he thought there must be something wrong with me."

"So, let's just summarise things so far - on the first night here you end up in Donald's bedroom, and on the second night here Staff B ends up in your bedroom. You're having a good trip so far, aren't you?"

Mum laughed as she said it, and I just shook my head and lay back down on the pillow. There was no point to defending myself when she was in such a silly mood.

"I think all the exercise is making you high," I said. "You're behaving like a drunk teenager. And actually, he told me about his time in the army and how he had to leave because his arm was blown off."

"Blown off?"

"Yep. I've got your attention now, haven't I? His arm was blown off by a landmine so he left. He has an artificial arm."

"Gosh, I've never noticed that before."

"No, but you remember how he always wears long sleeves and gloves? That's why."

"I want to hear more about this," said mum. "I'll have a shower after dinner instead of now. What else did he say?"

"Not much, to be honest. He said that when he left, he didn't know what he'd do with himself...all his family are soldiers and it's all he ever wanted to do. I think this place saved him."

"Gosh, that's incredible. Fancy losing your arm."

Mum had wandered towards the patio windows and was looking at the pool as she spoke.

"Makes you realise how grateful you should be, doesn't it?" she said.

We walked up to dinner together, both of us fantasising about the food that might be on offer. Mum thought it might be a gorgeous Italian meal, a lovely pasta dish with fresh lobster and freshly caught prawns. I said it would probably be a big steak and chips, or maybe a massive American burger with chips covered in chilli con carne.

"Shall we have a big bowl of nachos to start?" Mum said.

"Oh yes," I agreed. "And some of those salt and pepper calamari that are delicious. Maybe we should have a whole big selection of starters, before we get onto our main course."

"Good idea," said mum.

We got into the dining room, salivating with excitement at the thought of the food we had been discussing, then sat down and winced a little as they brought out a bowl of broccoli soup.

"At least it's not carrot," said Mum.

"Oh yes it is," said Abi, appearing beside us. "It's broccoli and carrot."

"Oh good," I said. "Exactly what we were both hoping for."

As soon as dinner was over, I wanted to go back to the room... I had visions of falling into an early sleep. Some of the guys talked about going for a walk, but that just felt like massive self-abuse. Why would you do more exercise? It baffled me.

"What are you up to tonight?" I asked Yvonne, who was sitting opposite me.

"I'm going to head off to the sauna again," she said, standing up and moving to leave the table.

"Actually, do you mind if I come with you?" said Simon, standing up as well.

I was intrigued as to how this would all pan out. I mean, if Yvonne was genuinely going to the gym and sauna and not just using it as an excuse to escape and see Staff A, she'd have no problem with Simon going along with her. I glanced at mum and we both awaited Yvonne's reply with some eagerness.

"Not this time Simon," said Yvonne. She smiled at him and left the room at top speed. Minutes later, I was chatting to mum, sitting just across from Staff A, when he jumped up.

"Right - I need to get off," he said. "See you all tomorrow."

With that, he left, and I turned to mum.

"Right, that's it. Something's definitely going on. Tomorrow night we're going to follow him," I said.

"Oooo...that does sound exciting," said mum. "But what if he sees us?"

"We'll just say we're going for a walk or something. I have to know what he's up to."

It wasn't long after the departure of the star-crossed lovers that the games started.

"I've got a fun game," said Donald, and though I'm usually completely up for late night games, I do like a few drinks inside me first. The prospect of playing silly 'tell all' games with strangers while completely sober was not in the least appealing.

Also, I was starving, and I know you're going to be cross with me for this, but I had a packet of crisps in my bag from the flight and I could fight off the urge to eat them no longer. More than anything in this world I wanted to go back, eat the crisps, have a shower and relax.

I managed to make it back without incident this time, going

straight to the right villa. Perhaps it was the lure of the crisps the sent me straight to the right place. I let myself in, rummaged through my bag which was tucked into the far corner of the wardrobe, and pulled out the crisps and a can of coke. Did I not mention that I had coke as well? Oh well, it's only a small can, hardly worth mentioning really.

Then I turned towards the patio doors. It was so hot in the room because mum had turned off the air conditioning when we left. I planned to sit outside in the moonlight and eat the crisps.

But then I saw something amazing...I blinked and checked again. My eyes hadn't mistaken me, there was someone in our pool doing synchronised swimming. It was quite mesmerising. I mean - the lady was really good. She was dressed in a 1950s-style costume and bathing cap and she kept bursting up out of the water, like they do, and kicking her golden legs high into the air while she was upside down. I opened the patio doors and stepped outside, walking as quietly as I could so as not to disturb her.

She didn't stop. She carried on flinging her legs in the air and shooting upwards out of the water with a nose clip on, hair scraped back into a bun, sparkly swimming costume, smiling wildly for an imaginary audience. She didn't see me but I watched her for a while. There was tinny music playing while she performed. She must be a competitive swimmer, she had a proper routine and everything.

"Mary, where are you?" came a voice from behind me. Mum was back. I rushed over to the shrub nearby and stuffed my crisps and coke into it, then ran back towards the villa.

"What are you doing out there?" she asked.

"Come out," I said. "I've just been watching this amazing synchronised swimmer in the pool."

"What?" said mum.

"Come and see," I insisted. "She's really good. She's got a sparkly costume on and everything."

Mum looked at me like I'd gone completely mad, but she followed me outside all the same. When we got there, the swimmer had gone...disappeared into the night with her tape recorder.

I looked at mum and could tell she didn't believe a word I was saying.

"She was here - she had a proper routine and the nose clip and everything, she was really good."

"OK," mum said.

"It's true. She was here."

"Maybe you shouldn't get so much sun tomorrow," she said.

"No, I promise you; I'm not going mad – she was there."

"You must have just seen the moonlight on the water," said mum.

"It wasn't moonlight on water, it was a synchronised swimmer," I insisted, but mum was turning to go back inside.

I'd try to convince her later, once I'd devoured my crisps. Once mum had disappeared into the villa, I rushed over to the shrub and crouched behind it to eat my illicit food. God it was amazing – the crisps tasted so incredibly flavoursome. Too flavoursome in a way - my lips were tingling and my head was buzzing. And the coke made my heart beat furiously. I felt great though. This was wonderful.

Then I heard mum's voice.

Shit.

"What are you doing now?" she asked.

"I'm just looking at this shrub," I said then, in a panic, I tipped the remainder of the crisps into my mouth. Mum had started to walk towards me. There was no way I could finish my mouthful before she got to me, but I didn't want to be caught with a mouthful of crisps. I flapped around, trying to work out what to do. I certainly wasn't going to spit them out – they were way too delicious for that. As mum got close, I freaked. I jumped up, ran to the pool and threw myself into the pool, fully clothed and with so many crisps in my mouth that my face looked like a puffer fish.

"Goodness Mary, I do worry about you," said mum. "I really think you should stay out of the sun as much as possible tomorrow."

I nodded and gave as much of a smile as I could without losing the crisps, and mum went back inside. I finished the crisps, clambered out of the pool and followed her, soaking wet, trying to work out how to explain my actions in such a way she wouldn't try to get me locked up in a lunatic asylum.

CHAPTER TEN: SHE FLOATS LIKE A
BUTTERFLY AND STINGS LIKE A BEE

"OK everyone, did you enjoy your breakfast?" asked Staff A, smiling and waiting for a response. I sat with my arms folded across my chest and looked around the room. We were a wildly disparate group - different ages, sizes, shapes and backgrounds, but I was fairly confident that we had one thing in common: none of us had enjoyed the Dickensian brown slop that had passed for breakfast. Thank God for the family bag of cheese and onion crisps that I had eaten behind the shrub last night (yes, it was a family bag - don't judge me).

"OK, no huge votes of approval for breakfast then," Staff A continued, having noticed the lack of his response to his enquiry about our food.

"In its favour: it was healthy and it will keep you full, and that's all that really matters. Now then, let's take a quick look at what we're going to be doing today."

I found myself staring at him as he spoke. He seemed to be directing all his comments to Yvonne. Or was that just my imagination? There was definitely a special bond between them. The question was - what bond? The way he'd acted with her at the airport - like long-lost friends...he seemed fascinated by her, but she had insisted she'd never met him before.

"Right," said Staff A, and he held up a blackboard full of activities for the day, detailing what had been arranged for us on the hour, every hour.

"I know it seems like a lot," he said, second-guessing what we were all thinking. "But I urge you to come to everything. As I keep saying, these few days will change your life, but only if you let them. My advice to you is to go with the flow. Stop stressing about not having as much food as you'd like and stop worrying about how hard the exercise will be - just do it. If you're struggling, stop, but don't not start. The worst thing you can do this week is to sit back and not participate. This is week is so short - it'll be gone in no time. If you work hard, you'll lose weight, feel great and have a whole new approach to life."

"That's right," said Staff B, joining 'A' at the front of the room. "I know we keep saying it, but you will get as much out of this week as you allow yourself to. It's day three - in some ways the hardest day. It's the course's 'hump day'. You'll get tired and you'll get hungry and you'll feel really frustrated, but you'll get through it and at the end of the week you'll look back and realise how much you can do if you try your hardest. This will act as inspiration when you get home. Does that make sense to everyone?"

There were murmurs of general agreement because what he said made perfect sense...it just all sounded very hard and I'd rather be lying by the pool eating crisps and watching the late-night synchronised swimmer.

First class of the day was combat skills. Blimey, they like their boxing here. This was the third class in which we'd been asked to don boxing gloves and hit one another. The third one!

Luckily, I'd missed the first two. On what planet do you need to do three boxing classes in two days, for God's sake?

We were told to get into pairs and I could see Donald approaching me - there was no way I was going with him. Mum immediately came skipping over to me assuming I'd be with her. This was something I wasn't very keen on at all. She's half my size and I'm half her age. That can't be a fair match-up, surely?

We were given gloves to put on - big, red gloves that you see proper boxers wearing. There was no part of this that seemed OK to me.

"Come on then," said mum, who had been to the two previous boxing classes and clearly thought she knew what she was doing. She danced around like she was Anthony Joshua or something. "Come and get me if you dare," she said.

I held my hands up in the boxing position and copied the stance that Staff B was demonstrating at the front of the class.

"A couple of light punches into your partner's gloves...let's see how you get on," he said.

Mum punched out so ferociously she sent my hands spinning away from my face.

"Gotcha," she said. Christ, she was tougher than she looked.

I shadow boxed back, avoiding hitting her with any force because I knew I'd hurt her.

"Come on, you can do better than that," said mum. "Show us what you're made of."

I continued to tap her gloves with mine and tried to make sure my technique was as good as possible, rather than putting all my power into the shots.

Staff A wandered over. "Is that all you've got?" he asked. "I'm sure you've got more power than that."

I didn't rise to the bait though, I just tapped gently. Then we swapped over again and it was mum's turn to hit. She didn't afford me anything like the same kindness. She whacked me ferociously...with every muscle she had. I swung my arms up to defend myself as the punches rained down on me.

"Now lots of little jabs," said Staff. "Punching as quickly and as hard as you can."

Oh hell. I lifted my arms up to protect myself from the onslaught that was bound to come my way. Mum really swung at me, as I shielded my face from the punches.

When we changed over, I just shadow boxed back.

"Come on, you can do better than that," said mum. "Come on, show us what you're made of."

What happened to the kindly mother who'd knitted me mittens and made me fish fingers for tea? This was a terrible development.

I continued to tap lightly on her gloves, showing admirable restraint while perfecting the noble art. Then Staff A charged over to us. He clearly didn't agree that restraint was a good idea. "I'm sure you've got more power than that."

I didn't rise to the bait, I just tapped gently. "Come on, Mary. The harder you hit, the leaner you'll be." I'm not sure whether this statement would stand up to rigorous scientific examination, but I got what he was saying...put more effort in. But the thing is I didn't want to hit my mum.

When the whistle went and we swapped over again, it was mum's turn to hit. She whacked me ferociously...Blimey. My hands went flying back and mum looked absolutely delighted with herself. Staff A applauded her.

"That's it," he said. "That's the way to do it."

The whistle went and we changed over for the final time. I was completely exhausted...punching was hard, but even standing there with your hands up, being punched, was hard work.

"Now then, come on Mary, you can do it," goaded Staff A, clapping his hands and urging me to put all my weight behind my punches. I swung out a little more than I had previously and, I don't know whether mum wasn't quite concentrating or had dropped her hands a bit, but my fist flew through and caught her right on her left eye with a tremendous thump.

"Ah," she screamed falling to the ground, holding her head. It was like it was all taking place in slow motion...mum spinning backwards, raising her hands to protect her face.

"Oh my goodness, what have you done?" said Staff A, rushing to mum's side, and glaring at me.

"I just did what you told me to do," I said. "In fact, I did what you told me to do when I knew very well that this was exactly what would happen, I should have trusted my own instincts."

I bent down next to mum who was telling me not to worry, and that everything was fine, but I could see her left eye was already starting to close up, and would no doubt go black overnight and leave her looking like she'd been street fighting.

"Let's get you back to the villa," said Staff A, lifting mum gently to her feet, and dropping his arm around her shoulder. I gathered mum's stuff together and ran after them, while the rest of the group stopped and stared at us.

Back at the villa, chef came out of the kitchen with an ice pack and asked what had happened.

"Mary punched her mum in the face," said Staff A.

"It wasn't quite like that," I said. "We were doing the boxing class and I just caught mum on the side of the face."

"Oh my goodness, what on earth made you punch her so hard?"

"I was just doing as I was told," I said. "When I wasn't punching very hard, I was told to hit harder."

"Yes, but not give your mum a black eye!" said Staff A. "No one told you to injure her."

"Are you OK, mum?" I said.

"Honestly, I'm absolutely fine. Please don't worry." But as

she looked up at me, her left eye was weeping and already looking swollen, I felt ill to the pit of my stomach.

"You should probably sit this next class out," said Staff A.

"Yes, sure, I think that's a good idea. Thanks," I replied. "I'll go back to my room for a lie down."

"Not you. Your mum," said Staff. "You should do the class; your mum should take it easy."

"Oh yes, of course."

There were two more classes after boxing, the first one to take place on the beach. Mum insisted on coming down with us, but instead of leaping around on the beach, she sat herself down on a rock, and watched as we did what Staff A called "sand training."

In case you were wondering, 'sand training' is when you do lots of activities that are hard enough on solid ground, but you do them on soft sand to make them so much harder.

Mum looked like such a sad, lonely figure, sitting there on the rocks, holding an ice pack to her face, but she insisted that she was OK, and just wanted to watch us. The others in the group had all gone up to her one by one to commiserate with her, and say how awful it was that she got hit in the face. With every comment of support she received, I felt like I was being indirectly castigated for my role in the whole thing.

"OK," said Staff A. "Welcome to "sand training". Can you all line up to face me please."

Staff A was standing with his back to the sea, allowing us to look over at the waves as they crashed down onto the beach while we worked out.

"Let's start with 20 jumping jacks, followed by 20 star jumps, run to Staff B and back, and repeat."

Oh God. This weight loss camp was just about doing the same tortuous exercises over and over again in different environments. Giving the sessions different names like 'sand training' 'hill training' and 'park work out' just allowed the trainers to convince us that we are doing lots of different things.

I was the last one back, of course. They were all running on the spot while they waited for me. I was exhausted already. I looked over at mum, longingly. I wish she'd punched me in the face instead.

Next it was burpees and running with high knees - we did one minute on, 30s off, for six minutes until I thought I might die of exhaustion. The knee lifts meant me whacking my knees into my enormous breasts that bounced around furiously inside my t-shirt even though I was wearing two bras.

After the aerobic exercise was over, I heaved a huge sigh of relief...until he said it was time for press ups, planks, holding squats and leg raises. I was soaking wet, thoroughly exhausted and - oddly - slightly exhilarated. Weird. I hated it, but I loved how it made me feel.

CHAPTER ELEVEN: MEETING TRACIE

It was time for lunch. THANK GOD. After we'd eaten, we would be having a talk from a visiting lecturer. The thought of a lecture was quite appealing, and I never imagined I'd be thinking that. But anything that involved sitting down rather than doing star jumps and press-ups was fine by me. And the afternoon activity was a long walk, so at least that shouldn't involve any heart attack-inducing bursts of energy.

Lunch was carrot sticks (I KNOW!!!), with a few pepper and cucumber sticks and a small bowl of homemade hummus.

While we ate, a tall, slim, ferociously heavily-tanned and heavily-made-up woman came in. She must have been mid-50s but was dressed like a young teenage girl, in brightest pink towelling shorts and a white t-shirt with white pom-pom socks inside wedge-heel trainers. Her hair was a bright, artificial blonde - almost white and down to her bottom and her lips were so inflated that they entered the room half an hour before the rest of her. And that's before we got onto the quite extraordinary breasts that looked like they belonged to a woman eight times her size.

It was as if she'd been beamed down from another planet. She looked like Barbie doll's heavily-tanned mum. We all sat there and stared, feeling wildly underdressed in our sweaty old tracksuits.

Staff A jumped up and went over to welcome her. I glanced at Yvonne, by far the most glamorous-looking woman in our midst, and followed her gaze as she took in the woman in front of us. Yvonne's face was an absolute picture. She didn't like this at all. I got the feeling that she didn't like Staff A being so attentive to the new arrival either. I was starting to believe that Staff A and Yvonne really were having an affair.

"OK, can I have your attention?" said Staff A. "I'd like to introduce you to Trace who is going to do a series of short talks about health and fitness issues that you can take back into your everyday lives with you. Tracie, over to you..."

There was a small burst of applause, leading Tracie to bow deeply, and unnecessarily. "Hiya, so I'm Tracie, and as you've been told I'm here to give you a few talks over the next few days, mainly about nutrition and the value of thinking about what you eat and not following fad diets, but also about exercise and why it's so vital that you bring regular movement into your lives."

"This could be hysterical," said mum, adjusting the ice pack on her eye so she could see Tracie properly. "There's no way she's a nutritionist."

"I know," I replied. "This could be really good fun."

We sat back in our seats. Out of the corner of my eye I could see Donald, staring at Tracie like a man possessed. His mouth had dropped open and a little drool had escaped from the side.

"The first thing I'd like to do is address some of the concerns that I know you'll have. Who is this woman before me? What does she know about food? I know I don't look like a nutritionist...I don't look wholesome and well-educated and as if I spend my time growing herbs and making healthy meals. That's because I don't...but I do know all about nutrition and I have lots of ideas for ways in which you can make your diet and your lifestyle healthier without too much effort.

"I was born in England but my mother is French, and when I was 13, we moved to France...people in France have a very difference approach to food, and I will be incorporating some of that thinking into my talks to you over the next few days."

She handed a pile of notes to Simon to hand out and I glanced at Donald who was still staring like some sort of maniac. I felt a pang of anger at his obvious interest in her. I thought he was supposed to fancy me? He was trying to get me to stay in his room one minute, but when a new woman arrived, he was all over her. Not that I was remotely interested, but - you know what it's like - it still smacks a bit when someone goes off you. I'd enjoyed being liked more than I'd realised, perhaps because it was so rare an occurrence.

"Are you OK?" Tracie asked Donald.

"I'm fine," he said, jolting himself out of his reverie and turning to look at the note that Simon had handed to him. "Absolutely fine."

"OK, well as you can see on the sheet, I believe strongly in movement. Not necessarily going to the gym or doing intensive cycling classes - just movement.

"I think one of the first things you need to do if you want to lose weight is to make your days as inefficient as possible. I know that sounds crazy but doing things less efficiently you'll build exercise and movement into your day. So - go the long way round to the bus stop, pace around while you're waiting for the kettle to boil.

"Most people in Europe sit still too much. Research shows clearly that those who move more, even if it's fidgeting or pacing around, are fitter and healthier than those who don't move.

"Let me tell you this - on average, obese people sit for two and a half hours more each day than lean people. In addition, lean people stand and walk for two hours a day more than obese people. How does that make you feel?"

She paused, waiting for someone to answer.

"I feel as if I ought to be fidgeting a bit more," I said. "You know - moving around."

"Yes. No one's saying you have to run a marathon every day or even continue to do the exercise classes that you're doing here today, but try to move more. If you're sitting down to watch tv, get up in the adverts and do a bit of tidying up or walk up and down the stairs a few times. If you've got a pile of three things to take upstairs take them one at a time. If you've got three bags of shopping in the boot - don't do that macho thing of trying to bring them all in at once - bring them in one at a time. Make your life more inefficient."

"This is better than I thought," mum whispered. "Make lots of notes for your blog."

"Oh yes, God - I forgot about the blog," I said, grabbing her pen off her and scribbling notes onto the side of the page. "Remind me every day. I have to start putting posts up as soon as I get back."

"OK, just a few other things to think about," said Tracie, she used her hands a lot when she spoke, displaying finger-nails that were about 4" long. Some of them were pierced and had jewels hanging from them. "There are the obvious things that you all know about - park as far away from the place you are going to as possible and walk the final bit, get off the bus a stop earlier, use the stairs rather than the escalators...you know - everyday things that make a real difference.

"Also, why not set the timer on your phone to bleep at 10 to the hour and get up and walk round for 10 minutes, then sit back down and carry on working? It'll make such a difference if you do that as often as you can through the day. Does that make sense?"

She seemed to look directly at me as she said it, so I nodded. It did make sense, to be honest. I knew I was never going to be a gym bunny, or someone who became obsessed with attending exercise classes regularly, but I could easily jump around for 10 minutes every hour. That's what I'd do. Everyone at work would be so impressed...if a little scared.

"OK," said Staff A. "We'll be hearing a lot more from Tracie over the next few days, we just wanted her to introduce herself and give you a range of things you can do at home to continue the good work you've done here. Now then - if anyone wants to take a comfort break, go now, and we'll head off on our three hour walk in 10 minutes. We'll be back in time for dinner."

CHAPTER TWELVE: LEARNING ABOUT WEIGHT LOSS

Mum and I wandered out of the villa onto the beautiful sun-dappled street outside, ready for our huge walk. It would have been so good to lie by the pool with a picnic but - no - more movement was demanded of us.

"What did you think of her?" I asked mum.

"She was better than I expected. I suppose I learnt a few things."

"The main thing I learnt, mum, is that if you have too much filler and too much of a boob lift, you'll look like Barbie."

The two of us cackled, then heard a sound behind us.

"Hello, how did you find my talk?"

Mum and I jumped and spun round to see Tracie standing there. Hopefully she hadn't heard us talking. From the smile on her face it didn't look like it.

"It was great," said mum. "Really good."

"Yes, very useful," I agreed. "Just what we needed."

I noticed she'd changed into proper trainers and was no

longer wearing the platform shoes she'd been in earlier. Happily, the bobble socks remained.

"Christ, what happened to you?" she said to mum.

"Oh, that's nothing," said mum. "It's just where Mary hit me."

Tracie looked at me in disbelief, waiting for an explanation.

"I didn't hit her," I said for what felt like the 100th time that day. "I accidentally caught her on the side of her face in a boxing class earlier today. That's all."

"Oh dear. I hope it gets better soon. You'll have a real shiner there," said Tracie, taking my arm and mum's arm and pulling us close. "I want to walk along with you girls."

We followed behind the throng of bodies ahead of us, turning a sharp left to go down the concrete steps onto the beach. It really was a very stunning place... such an open, welcoming beach. As soon as you emerged from the stone stairs, there it was in front of you - the magnificent sea, painted the loveliest blue as if in a van Gogh painting, and miles of sand, fringed with cliffs at the far side. The sky was the colour of dreams - not a cloud in sight, and no sound of anything but the gentle lapping of the water. And, to be fair, the whole place looked much more beautiful when you didn't have to do star jumps and burpee jumps on the sand.

"Come on you lazy buggers, speed up," said Staff A, completely ruining the whole atmosphere.

"Is this what you do full-time?" I asked Tracie. "Going round to these camps lecturing on exercise?"

"I run my own company," she said. "It's health and fitness based, with some personal coaching thrown in. I'm based locally, and work with a number of sports teams and exercise companies."

"Personal coaching - that's exactly what I need," I said. "I just find it so hard not to eat stuff that's bad for me."

"It's not your fault, dear," said mum. "The amount of fat and sugar they put into food these days - it's hard to avoid it. It's really not your fault."

"Oh, but it has to be," said Tracie, stepping over a small sandcastle. "You have to take responsibility, it's the only way."

"How can she take responsibility when manufacturers shove a load of rubbish into food," said mum defensively.

"Don't buy it," replied Tracie. "If a manufacturer sells a product with loads of fat and sugar in it, and you buy it, and get fat. Whose fault is it?"

We walked along without answering her.

"Ultimately, it's your fault," she said. "And if you try to remember that, life will be much easier for you."

"How?" asked mum.

"Because the manufacturers are trying to sell food to you to make a profit. That's their job. That's what they are there for. And they know that the better the food tastes, the more of it people will buy and the more profits they will make. It has to be your job to check whether eating these products is doing you any good or not. We can put pressure on manufacturers to be more honest with us, but at some stage you've got to be honest with yourself, and realise that what they want to achieve and what you want to achieve are polar opposite things. They want you to eat loads of it; you need to stop eating it. How are we going to stop you from eating it?"

Neither me nor mum replied.

"Well, one obvious way is by arming you with all the information you need to make sensible decisions around food. Shall I bore you with some facts and figures, or would you rather me shut up so we can concentrate on walking?"

We were heading up a hill and though I knew there would be magnificent sights when we got up there, it was tough walking and I didn't want to think about it anymore than I had to. "Facts and figures please," I said. These would be useful for my blog posts too.

"OK," she said. "Britain is the fattest country in Europe; it's a problem. But a recent Tory party conference was sponsored by Tate and Lyle. Now, think about that for a minute. If the government is so entranced by money that it can't see the damage that sugar is doing to the population, who's looking out for you? I'll tell you who - you. It has to be you who looks after you: not companies, not the government – you.

"One in three children under 15 is overweight or obese and things are getting worse. Companies are targeting kids from a very young age with sugar, salt and fat. Only you can stop it. Only you can say 'no - I'm not going to eat that stuff, I'm going to be strong and healthy and eat natural foods that are good for me."

"Yeah," I said. I knew she was right but I was so exhausted I could hardly think, let alone speak. Tracie seemed to be prac- tically skipping up the hill, oblivious to how steep it was. She wasn't remotely out of breath.

"You know what I was saying earlier about doing bits of exercise through the day? Well - you have to do that. YOU. If you don't, you'll get fatter and fatter. Companies are making it as easy as possible for you to access their food.

"Food is being delivered to our doors. Dominoes pizzas and all those lovely big Chinese takeaways - being handed to us on our doorsteps. It's the complete and absolute opposite of how we were meant to consume food. Human beings were designed to go out and hunt for food. You didn't get food without physical exertion first and that was how the body was designed to work.

"Now the most physical thing you have to do is open the door. It just isn't any good for us, you need to try and make yourself walk around, walk to the pizza place at the very least!

"Another interesting fact for you - research shows that the

more takeaways there are in an area, the more of it you will eat. It's the same with all addictions, the more readily available alcohol is the more problems people have with drinking. It's a very straightforward thing, but you have to control it. No one else will.

"Avoid takeaways, don't go anywhere near them. Don't tell yourself that you'll just have a healthy dish, keep away from them altogether.

"Think about your body in terms of what it was designed for. It really doesn't want to be crammed full of fatty food and no exercise. It doesn't thrive like that. It won't last a long time like that. Next time you see a really old person, look at what size they are. They'll be thin. Very old people are always thin because fat people die younger. That's how simple and straightforward it is. It's not at all healthy to be fat."

We'd reached the top of the hill where the others were all waiting for us, looking down on the beautiful scenery below. You could see for miles - out to sea where boats were bobbing on the water and right across to the other side of the cliffs. I breathed in the warm air and thought about how there was every chance that I'd die before getting down again. I didn't want to be fat, it wasn't like I was deliberately eating to get fat, I just was fat. It was as much a part of me as my slightly wonky eyebrows or the small scar at the top of my thigh.

"Have you always struggled with your weight?" asked Tracie.

"No - I used to be really thin and really fit. I was a gymnast when I was a girl and trained all the time."

"Oh wow," said Tracie, clearly amazed that there was ever a time when I would dance around in a leotard. "How did you find gymnastics?"

"Quite cruel," I said. "It's a relentless pursuit of perfection. It's a tough sport."

"Yes, the performance sports are," said Tracie with a

knowing smile. She'd probably been a dancer or something in her day.

"Portugal's very beautiful, isn't it?" said mum. "I never realised just how lovely it was." She turned to Tracie: "Have you lived here long?"

"No, I was born in England and lived in France when I was a girl," she said. "I didn't come to Portugal until I was in my 20s... chasing a man. An Englishman."

"Ah, that's why you're English is so good," said mum. "I'm always very jealous of people who can speak more than one language."

"You should learn then," said Tracie. "Teach yourself Portuguese, it's very easy."

"I'm too old to learn new things," said mum, sitting down onto the grass, and urging us to join her. Bottles of water were being passed round, so we waited patiently for them to reach us.

"I find I get so tired very easily. Once I turned 65, everything became difficult."

"Are you sleeping OK," asked Tracie. She sat down next to mum and arranged her glossy orange legs in such a way that you could see right up her towelling shorts to where her knickers would have been, if she'd have been wearing any. I noticed with dismay that the orange tan colour didn't stop at the top of her thigh, but continued all the way up.

"No, not really. I just get over-tired, I think. However much I do during the day, I never sleep much. Even on this holiday, Mary's been going to bed before me.

"Sleep's important," said Tracie. "There are lots of things you can do to get a better night sleep. The main thing to start with is a sleep diary, just so you know exactly how much sleep you're getting. Then try going to bed and waking up at roughly the same time each day, that way your body will get used to it, it will fall into a rhythm and you'll fall asleep faster and wake up easier.

"The other thing to do is to swing open the curtains and let the light in first thing in the morning, and take a brisk walk whenever you can. Doing four 30- to 40-minute walks a week helps people with insomnia sleep longer."

"I don't think I can really be bothered," said mum. "I'm OK really, you know."

"Oh no, you must. One large study that followed participants over a 5- to 10-year period found that people who slept less than 7 hours a night were more likely to be obese."

I smiled at her. "Do you have a handy study to quote for every occasion, or do you sometimes make it up?" I said.

"Ha, ha," she said. "I have read lots of studies and I've been giving talks on this subject for 20 odd years. I promise you, I'm not making them up."

We were told to get to our feet and run a little on the spot to get our limbs moving again.

"Shall I give you one tip that will change your life for the better?" said Tracie.

Mum and I looked at one another. "That would be nice," said mum. "Would your advice be - don't ever go to a boxing class with your daughter?"

Tracie smiled. "Maybe that would be a good idea, but my main piece of advice to you, and I suspect this will be more for Mary - make sure you have 60 whole minutes without electronic devices every day. That's no phone, computer, television - nothing. For an hour. If you do that, you will see your health improve, your mood improve and - eventually - your fitness improve."

"Right," I said. "I can't imagine that."

"No, but you should. You'd be amazed at how your mind calms and your stress recedes. You'll have a whole hour free every day...you could read, have a bath, go for a walk, meditate or do all of them."

"I'll try," I said, but in many ways what she was suggesting would be harder than anything else we'd done. A whole hour? Even at work I didn't go for more than 10 or 15 minutes without a cheeky text from one of my friends, or a sneaky look on Facebook. I'd try though, I just couldn't imagine how successful I'd be.

CHAPTER THIRTEEN: WHY DO WE NEED TO WALK SO MUCH?

Aﬆer the lecture from Tracie, I tried not to use my phone for the rest of the walk. I didn't play music or snapchat as I went along, I just enjoyed looking at nature. Blimey, the time dragged. Not because of the nature - the place was beautiful, just because I'm used to walking and talking at the same time as texting and messing around playing games. It felt like the walk went on forever without my phone to distract me.

When we got back, half of us collapsed in the sitting room area of villa one, and the other half decided that enough wasn't quite enough and started swimming in the pool. No need to tell you which half I was in. I lay slumped in the armchair next to mum who looked utterly exhausted. Her eye patch had slipped a little revealing a very red, very closed-up eye beneath it.

"That's the end of your formal exercise for today," said Staff B, standing up before us. "Obviously, if you want to do more, go ahead." He indicated outside, where the bunch of 10 or more nutters were racing up and down the pool. "Tracie's offered to answer any health or fitness questions you may have, but other than that, you're free to go, and I'll see you for our penultimate dinner tonight."

Tracie stood up. "This is nothing formal, but if you do have any questions, I'd be very happy to answer them," she said.

"Why the hell are we doing so much walking?" said a small guy with little round glasses. I'd seen him at some of the classes and he struck me as being very fit. "There seems to be an extraordinary amount of it. I walk every day at home, but just for 40 minutes at a time."

"Good question," I said, nodding enthusiastically.

"OK," said Tracie. "Well - it's a good way to see the place. Obviously, we're in a lovely part of the world...many of you haven't been here before and won't come here again, so it's good to take time out to look around and see things. But in terms of fitness, the answer is very simple - the reason we walk so much is because walking is exceptionally good for you."

"I bet she's got a study that proves it," I whispered to mum.

"Let me prove this to you," said Tracie, and mum and I did a secret high five. "Let me prove to you that walking can save your lives."

"Save our lives?"

"Yep," she said. "Does anyone know why?"

"Because you get your heart rate going, and your limbs moving?" I ventured.

"Star pupil. Well done," said Staff B, moving to stand next to Tracie. Staff B was quite pale, and when he stood next to her it threw into stark relief just how orange she was.

I looked up to catch mum's eye but she was looking through the patio windows, watching the seagulls dance elegantly through the sky over the pool, straining to watch them with her one good eye.

"Sorry to interrupt you Tracie, but we forgot to give out

your snacks earlier, so I'll hand them out to you now, while you're listening," said Staff B.

"Oh My God - that's the greatest news ever," I blurted out, rather too loudly, encouraging titters of laughter from those assembled. It suddenly dawned on me that the group here were the rebels of the course, the kids on the back seat of the bus, the ones flicking bits of paper at the teacher. The well-behaved kids were outside doing extra homework.

It was quite a jolly moment.

Then I was handed half an apple. HALF AN APPLE! And my mood bombed.

"Since I'm a star pupil, can I have a whole apple?" I tried.

"Nope."

Blimey these people didn't know the meaning of the word 'snack' they should see me hoovering nachos while watching Netflix.

"OK, the importance of walking," continued Tracie. She had turned down her half of an apple. She said she didn't want to ruin her dinner. "I need to start by telling you a story...a story about bus drivers and bus conductors."

This wasn't the most promising of starts to a story, but I decided to bear with it.

"In 1949, Jerry Morris, a professor of social medicine in London, conducted a study to compare the rates of heart disease between London bus drivers and conductors. "The drivers and conductors were from similar social backgrounds; however, there was a marked difference in the rates of illness between them.

"Morris's study showed that conductors were half as likely to die from a heart attack as drivers. He wanted to know why. In the end, he concluded that it was because in every working day, while drivers were typically sedentary, conductors walked all day.

"So, it was more than 50 years ago that doctors realised that regular exercise through the day was a life saver."

"Gosh, is that right? That's really interesting," said Simon.

"Yes - it's very interesting because the difference between the drivers and the conductors and their life expectancies was so stark. Back then there were just two people working on every bus - a driver who sat in his seat all day and drove, and a conductor who scrambled around - up and down the stairs, making his way among passengers, and collecting fares at every stop.

"Seeing the results and working out why, was one of the first times that doctors began to appreciate the link between early death and an inactive, sedentary life. Being overweight or obese wasn't taken much into account back then as most people were of normal weight. The drivers in the study weren't any more or less overweight than the conductors. Now, a half century later, the link between a sedentary life and early death has been reconfirmed in dozens of studies worldwide.

"Exercise is important...not just for weight loss or toning or anything like that, but for living. If you want to live a long and healthy life, exercise has to be a cornerstone of that. Walking is excellent exercise. That's why we do so much of it on the course."

She paused at this stage, as if giving us all time to take in the magnitude of what she was saying. A silence fell over us. I'd definitely try and walk more when I got back. I could easily get off the bus early or something...be more like the conductor than the driver.

"Any more questions?" she asked.

I had one. I always have questions: "You said when we were talking before that manufacturers were putting loads of sugar in our foods and we needed to make sure we didn't buy it.

Why do they do that? Surely if they just made food healthier, a lot of the western world's problems would go away?"

"Yes, but their priority isn't trying to solve the problems of the western world. You are talking about commercial companies, trying to make money, and they sell more food if it's laced with sugar and fats. The reason that didn't happen in the past is because we have different tastes today.

"The reason for this? And one of the big problems of modern living? Freezers. Yep. More than 95% of people have freezers in the UK, and much of the food that we put in the freezer has to be highly processed in order for it to survive the process. Doing this removes flavour, so then you have to add in more sugar, salt and fat to get the flavour back and make them taste nice again. In the past people just ate fresh food and bought fresh every day, because they didn't have freezers so they had to. We were much healthier without them. The healthiest way to live is to buy fresh food every day."

Again, she paused, and I looked at mum who was trying to fix her eye-patch. Simon leaned over as if to lend a hand, but I batted him away before he could help. "I've got this, thanks," I snarled, as he retreated.

"Everything OK?" asked Tracie.

"Oh yes, completely fine," said mum. "I'm really enjoying listening to you. Do carry on."

"OK - well, just one final point about processing food is that it makes the food easier for the body to digest. Do you remember what I was saying earlier about making life as difficult for yourself as possible? Making yourself use energy whenever you can? Well, the same applies here - normally you have to use energy to break up the food that you eat. The body has to break up the various components and work hard to digest it, and a certain percentage of the calorific contact of the food is used up doing this.

"But if all the work has been done for you in the processing, then all the calories in the product go straight into your body without you expending any of them in breaking it down, so food is more calorific as a result.

"You need to eat healthy, unprocessed food whenever you can."

"What? Never use the freezer?"

"I don't have one. I don't think they're a good idea," said Tracie. "But if you've got a large family and rely on them, the tip is just to make sure you eat fresh, healthy, unprocessed food as much as you can, and only use the freezer for emergencies.

There was a lot of mumbling at this...a lot of displeasure at the thought of not being able to pull burgers out of the freezer and shove them straight into the oven at tea-time.

"Any more tips?" asked Donald.

"I think that's about it for now," she said. "There will be more time to talk tomorrow."

"OK, so there's nothing else you do to keep yourself looking so fit and...if you don't mind me saying...amazing, that we should be doing?"

"Oh goodness, thank you," said Tracie, blushing a little through her radiant orange skin. "I do take a low dose aspirin daily. That's not a bad idea as you get older. It's controversial, I know, and I wouldn't advise taking drugs for the sake of it, but a blood thinning medicine like aspirin helps to prevent heart attacks and strokes. My sister had a stroke a few years ago, and I was classified as high risk, so I take one every day. Aspirin makes the blood less sticky and helps to prevent heart attacks and strokes. One with breakfast dramatically reduces the risks."

CHAPTER FOURTEEN: BUM FLASHING

Dinner on the penultimate evening was slightly better (but we're coming from quite a low point). Instead of the usual bowl of indescribably bad soup, we had salmon with broccoli and even a yoghurty thing for dessert which tasted quite sweet and delicious. It was served in a tiny bowl the size of an egg cup, of course, so when I'd eaten it, I ran my finger round the inside of the bowl, trying to get every last morsel out. Then I tried to put my tongue into it to make sure there was nothing left, but mum took it off me and told me to behave.

After dinner, there was the usual bee-line for the sofas and the commencement of the games. It was like living in the past, in the days before televisions. But none of that bothered me because I was entertaining myself by watching Yvonne and, as always, she got to her feet and said that she was leaving for the spa down the road.

I looked at mum. I wasn't sure whether she'd want to come on this expedition with me, given how exhausted she looked, and given that her eye was now completely closed up and a rather unattractive shade of grey. But I thought I'd try anyway.

"Come on, Yvonne's gone - let's sneak out and follow her. I'm dying to know where she goes," I said, nudging her.

"Wouldn't it be nicer to sit here and drink herbal tea with the others?" she replied.

"No," I replied, honestly. "Why would you want to do that when you could be launching yourself into the night on an extraordinary expedition."

"Really?" said mum. "An 'extraordinary expedition' to see whether Yvonne is meeting up with Staff A? Good job you don't work for the secret service, you'd be blown away by the things they have to do."

"Are you coming or not?" I said, not dignifying her comment with an answer.

"Okay," she said wearily. "But only so I'm there to keep an eye on you if anything goes wrong."

"Fair enough," I said. "I wish I had camouflage gear with me, and a head torch."

"Oh God," said mum. "Let's go."

We left the villa, claiming tiredness and said we were heading off to get an early night, but turned left at the top on the street, and took the road to the stone steps which led down onto the beach, rather than back to our villa.

"How do we know where to go?" asked mum. "We can't go to every bar in town."

"I don't think there are many bars," I replied. I did a recce by talking to Abi and she said there were three cafes and a hotel. The hotel is where the gym and spa are, and where Yvonne claims she goes. Let's start there."

"OK," said mum. "But I can't go in like this, can you put my patch back on my eye for me. I'll scare everyone."

I helped mum to apply the cotton pad and large plaster, and we continued on our way.

"I'm going to have a glass of wine tonight," I said. "Just a small one."

"Really? What, and undo all the good work? Why don't you just have a glass of water like I'm going to."

"Because I really want a glass of wine. Come on I've been so good all the way through - I haven't had any sneaked in snacks or anything..." (ssshhhhhh....no need to mention the three packets of crisps - mum doesn't need to know).

"OK, but just have a small one," said mum. We walked along the beach towards the seafront cafes, and I scanned the area as we went - looking out for Yvonne and Staff A. I didn't even know whether Staff had followed her this time because he hadn't been in dinner tonight, but I suspected he had. I peered out, watching for every movement. I felt like a fugitive avoiding arrest.

"There it is," I said, pointing to a large hotel which looked as if it had lovely views of the sea. It was very plush. I imagined that it would probably have a very nice spa.

"What are you going to do?" asked mum.

"Well, why don't we go in and see whether they are in the bar?"

"OK," said mum. "Of course, Yvonne could be in the spa and Staff A could be in his room doing press ups or something."

"Yes, I realise that," I said. "But unless we go and check things out, we'll never know."

"We should look in the spa first," said mum. She'd obviously worked out that any investigation headed up by me would attempt to start in the bar.

"Or the main bar," I tried. "We could have a quick drink while making a plan?"

"No - spa first. That's where she said she was going so we should check that out. Then, if she's not there, we'll know she lied and can try and find her."

"OK," I said, quite impressed that mum had thought this through so carefully.

First, we walked into the gym, and pretended we were hotel guests taking a look round. There was no sign of either Yvonne or Staff A in there. It was a nice place. Very plush, with lots of equipment, screens flashing on every machine and music sweeping through the place.

There weren't many people there, and those who were there didn't seem to be doing a great deal, it was more the sort of gym you were seen in rather than one you worked out in.

"OK, she's not here," I said to mum, stating the bleeding obvious. "Let's check out the spa area."

So, we walked out of the gym and into the spacious, pine changing room - it looked and smelled like a giant sauna. There were steam rooms, jacuzzi, saunas and 'splash pool' leading off the main changing room - each one was behind a door. There was a big pile of fluffy towels outside each of the doors.

"You'll have to get undressed, you can't walk into the steam room like that," said mum, flicking her hand to illustrate my inappropriate clothing.

"Damn," I muttered. This was all getting to be quite hard work.

I slipped off my leggings and t-shirt and went to wrap one of the lovely soft, fluffy towels around me. Of course, it was far too small and didn't come near to covering me. I grabbed another one and tried to arrange the two of them so that I wouldn't expose myself to everyone in the steam room. Then I went in. The place was full of steam - which, I guess, is what I was expecting, but I hadn't thought through the fact that I wouldn't be able to see anyone in there. I sat down and waited for my eyes to adjust. There was just one woman in there. Considerably older than Yvonne. On to the next room. The sauna was easier to see in - three women, no Yvonne. Then I walked into the room marked splash pool.

"I'll come with you," said mum. "I can go in here in my

clothes." She followed me through the door which led to two small swimming pools. The glass roof had been opened so it was like being outside. There were about 20 people there - some swimming but most of them lounging on sunbeds and reading or talking. Clutching my towels tightly, I walked around, checking each face in turn to see whether Yvonne was there. No. No sign of her. So, I walked back to the door, reaching to push it open so we could go back into the changing room. But reaching out for the door involved letting go of my towel, before I could stop it, the first towel had fallen to the ground, quickly followed by the second one.

Oh God.

My rather large bottom was exposed to all of the splash pool users in the lovely Portuguese spa.

"Put it away, Mary," mum said, under her breath.

CHAPTER FIFTEEN: WHEN MOUTH-TO-MOUTH GOES WRONG

Ⅰ got changed as quickly as possible and tried to forget about the fact that everyone in the spa had seen my bum.

"They weren't looking. No one noticed," mum kept saying, in an effort to reassure me. But I'd seen the looks of horror and heard the gasps as my towel hit the floor.

"I'll definitely need a glass of wine now," I said, as we walked into the hotel bar.

"I thought that might be the case," said mum.

I didn't loiter when we entered the bar. I walked straight up and ordered a large glass of wine for me and sparkling water for mum, then took a massive swig out of it and almost reeled from the power of the taste. I'd drunk nothing but water and three cans of coke since I arrived in the country. The taste of wine almost knocked me off my feet.

"Gosh, these small glasses are big, aren't they?" I said to mum, indicating the size of my large glass. "I'm glad I didn't have a large one."

"Golly, yes," said mum. "There's no way you'll be able to drink all that."

Does she know nothing about me at all?

"Come on - let's take a wander and see whether we can find them. I know you won't relax until you've seen them," said mum, taking a delicate sip out of her glass

We walked around, cautiously looking for Staff A and Yvonne. In my head, the plan was for us to see them, but for them not to see us. I hadn't quite worked out how we were going to do this. I realised it would probably involve me throwing myself behind a pillar or a pot plant.

We walked around a couple of times, looking into all the nooks and crannies. I even went into the ladies to check, and stood for an unseemingly long time outside the gents.

Nope. They weren't there.

"We'll drink these then go to the other little bars on the beachfront," I said. "If they're not in any of those, then they are not in town tonight."

Mum smiled and shook her head at me. I know she thought I was mad, but it was quite intriguing the way they sneaked out like that. And I didn't believe that they'd never met before this holiday, the way he reacted to her at the airport was straight out of Love Story.

We took our glasses over to a table near to the window. All of the tables around us were full of people chatting in groups, enjoying food and drink. There were bowls of fries, oven baked brie and piles of chicken wings on the table next to me. I was dying to reach over and take one, but I managed to control myself.

I just watched them instead. Staring at the woman as she put a potato skin, loaded with cheese and bacon into her mouth.

"Stop looking like that," said mum.

"I can't help it." I replied. "It's torture sitting here next to them."

The woman eating the potato skin was English, as was

everyone else in the group. They chatted about people they knew from home and what they were up to. And I relaxed as the familiar sounds of people discussing Love Island and Brexit washed over me. I was starting to really enjoy my evening away from the camp.

Then, suddenly, the women I'd been studying started having a coughing fit. She fell to the ground in a dramatic fashion, holding her chest. She looked in considerable pain, but no one at her table did anything, they just looked around at each other. The woman writhed on the floor - reaching up to them, as if to indicate that she needed help.

I'd done a first aid course a few years ago, so fancied my chances of keeping her heart going until the ambulance came. I jumped out of my seat and ran over to her, aggressively turning her onto her side and opening her airway to check whether she was breathing. I tipped her neck back and prepared to give her mouth-to-mouth.

"Call an ambulance," I shouted to mum.

I felt amazing. Invincible. I was Wonder Woman. I'd be in every national newspaper and probably on that morning TV show with Piers Morgan. I'd definitely go to Downing Street and meet the Prime Minister.

I leaned in to give the woman mouth-to-mouth and save her from certain death when she suddenly pushed me away dramatically. She used quite a lot of force for a woman who'd been at death's door two minutes ago. Then she sat up and wagged her finger at me: "What are you doing? Get off me."

"I thought you were having a heart attack or something. I was trying to help," I said. I was alarmed and confused at the odd reaction that my kind act had provoked.

"We're playing a murder mystery game and you're completely ruining it."

"Oh sorry," I said. "I thought you were in trouble."

"No. We picked names out of a hat earlier and I'm the victim. I have to die. It's part of the game"

"Oh, I see. I'm sorry," I repeated, as a couple more people joined their table.

"Oh, my goodness," said one of them. "That's the flasher from the spa."

Everyone on the table was now staring at us. Mum looked completely baffled. I don't think she knew what was going on.

"Come on, we're going," I said. Mum stood up and the two of us spun round and walked dramatically away from the table...just as Staff A and Yvonne walked through the door.

"Hit the floor!" I shouted to mum, as if a gun-wielding terrorist had just entered the building. We both fell to our knees and crawled back under the table of the group whose game I'd just wrecked.

"What the hell is she up to now?! I heard one of them say.

Staff and Yvonne walked to the bar.

"Quick, let's go," I said to mum, and the two of us speed crawled to the exit, darted out and ran down the road, not stopping until we reached the beach.

"God that was fun," I said to mum.

"No, that was ridiculous. Everyone in there thinks we're insane."

"But at least we know that they are definitely having an affair," I said to mum.

"Unless they are just friends?" she suggested.

"But then why would they sneak out, and why would she lie about where she was going?"

Mum shrugged, as we walked back over the sand towards the stone steps. "It's odd, isn't it? You just wouldn't have put those two together - they seem such different people."

"I know. I think that's what's so intriguing. I bet he flew her out here specially to see her. I'm glad we came down to find out. And thanks for coming with me," I said. "It would have been horrible if I'd gone by myself."

"No problem my little flasher," she said, laughing as she said it. "Honestly, you should have seen their faces when your towel dropped. They were a picture."

"I thought you said no one saw…"

"Ah, yes - I lied about that. They all saw," she said. And we both burst out laughing.

My legs were really aching by the time I got back to the villa. It had been an action-packed evening: flashing, ruining a party game, then crawling out of the pub on hands and knees.

"Why do the oddest things always happen to me?" I asked mum, forlornly. "Other people manage to go through days without punching their mother in the face or anything. I wish I could be like other people. Did they really see my bottom in the sauna? That's so embarrassing."

Mum burst into laughter, and before long I was laughing too. "It really was the most ridiculous evening, wasn't it?" she said through spluttering laughter, as she gave me a hug and sat down on the bed next to me. "Honestly…"

Then she gasped and pointed outside. Her mouth was wide open. I followed her finger and there - in our pool again - was the synchronised swimmer. She danced merrily through the water while the two of us sat on my bed watching her.

"She's really good, isn't she?" I said.

"Yes," said mum. "She's wonderful. I thought you'd lost your mind, talking about women dancing in the pool. But look at her - she's there and she's really good. Let's go and watch her from the poolside."

Mum undid the back door and the two of us walked onto the patio. The same music was playing as last time I'd seen her - gently drifting through the night air as she danced around.

She pushed herself up out of the water effortlessly as we walked towards the pool, but as we got close the same thing happened...she saw up and swam towards the edge, leapt up onto the side with considerable agility, and ran away, tearing off her sparkly swimming hat to reveal a streak of blonde hair, grabbing her music player and disappearing into the trees.

"Oh, that's such a shame," said mum, looking really disappointed. "I wanted to watch her."

"I know, mum. Me too. Oh, hang on. She's dropped something," I walked to the edge of the pool and there lay her swimming hat...it was very old-fashioned with small flowers on it, and not sparkly at all. It must have been the reflections of the moonlight off the water catching it as she danced that had made it look as if it was covered in sequins.

I carried the hat back to where mum was waiting. Inside the cap, the initials NSF/TM were sewn.

"I need to take it back to her," I said to mum.

"Well, leave it here - she's bound to come back when she realises she left without it."

"No - I mean I want to find her - I want to know about her."

"Oh God," said mum, seeing the excitement burning in my eyes. "We don't have time for more spying missions. When are you going to go off and find her? Tomorrow is the last day."

"I'll go in the morning," I said. "I'm not doing boxing and combat training for three hours, that's for sure. I'm lethal."

"You're not lethal," said mum.

"Really? Have you looked in the mirror recently?"

Mum shook her head and climbed into bed. "I'm just thrilled that a synchronised swimmer really exists and you're not barking mad."

I lay back on my bed, still holding the cap, my mind spinning with thoughts and plans about how I might find the mystery swimmer.

As I lay there in the darkness, unbeknownst to me, the lady came back and, silently, while mum and I slept, she scoured the garden looking for her cap. She looked through the shrubs and moved the sunbeds and deck-chairs around, but it was nowhere to be found. Disappointed, she left, off into the night from whence she came

CHAPTER SIXTEEN: IN SEARCH OF THE PHANTOM SYNCHRONISED SWIMMER

I woke up the next morning for our final full day in camp still holding onto the swimming cap. It took me a few moments to remember what the odd item in my hand was. I had clutched it all night, leaving my palm sweaty underneath its rubbery skin. I felt a wave of excitement when I saw it, and shot out of bed still gripping onto it. Today was the day when I would find synchro woman.

I went over to where my phone was plugged into the wall, near the dressing table on the other side of the room and typed in Google to begin investigating. It was only 5am - earlier than I'd been up all week. It came as no surprise to me at all that when there was the prospect of physical exercise, I had absolutely no desire to get out of bed; but when there was a mysterious synchronised swimmer to locate I was out of bed faster than you could say 'nose clip'.

Mum slept soundly beside me while I put the initials embroidered into the cap into Google, hoping that the letters would mean something; that they would reveal where the swimmer had come from. NSF/TM: the letters had to be the name of a swimming club or something.

But...Nope. Nothing. Next, I googled synchronised swimming clubs in the area but I couldn't find anything. This sleepy region of Portugal was not awash with sporting amenities, certainly not of the water dancing kind, but synchro woman must be based locally, surely. I couldn't believe the woman came miles to use my pool. That made no sense at all.

There was a sports centre with a swimming pool in the area and it seemed to be a short bus ride away, so I figured that would probably be my first stop. There must be someone there who could tell me where synchronised swimming classes were held in the area. They might even be listed on the sports centre's website but it was impossible to tell by looking at it because it was all in Portuguese; no English at all.

I worked out that I could get the bus from outside the beachfront cafes. It was only a few stops.

As I studied the bus route, I heard a small movement behind me as mum woke up. "Goodness, what are you doing up so early?" she asked.

"Trying to work out how to find the synchronised swimmer," I said.

"Mind if I put the light on?".

"Of course not. I was only sitting in the dark so I didn't wake you."

Mum switched on the light by her bed and I looked over at her.

"Oh. My. God," I screamed. "Oh Christ."

"What?" Mum looked perplexed.

"Your eye!" I said. "It looks like you've been in a fight with Mike Tyson...and lost."

Her eye was black and completely sealed up. It was puffy and tender looking. It really did look like a boxer's eye the day after a fight.

"Oh, then it must look worse than it feels," said mum. "It actually it's a lot less painful today than it was yesterday."

"I think you need to see a doctor," I said. "Do you want to come with me today on a hunt for Synchro Woman and we'll find a doctor?"

"I'm sure there's no need," said mum. "And if this is your way of co-opting me into a chase around the country looking for someone whose face we've never seen and whose name we don't know, you can forget it."

"No, I'm being serious mum," I said (and I was). "I'll forget the hunt for the synchronised swimmer - we'll just go and get you to a doctor. We should have gone yesterday. Honestly, it looks really bad."

"But surely the people on the course would have suggested a doctor if they thought I needed one."

"Yeah, you'd think so," I said. "But they're all army people, you could probably lose a leg and they'd get you to hop through the exercises. They don't do 'injuries'."

"I suppose so," she said. "But it doesn't feel too bad at all. I'm sure in a couple of days it'll be perfect."

"But what if it's not? What if it's infected and you lose an eye and have to walk around wearing an eye patch for the rest of your life? Won't you wish you'd been to see a doctor then?"

"Yes, I suppose," she said. "And I can't really do three hours of combat training this morning anyway, can I? Let's go and find a doctor."

"Good, I'll see if google knows where the nearest one is," I said.

"And I suppose we might as well make some initial enquiries about the synchronised swimmer while we're out and about. I know how keen you are."

"Oh good," I said, rubbing my hands together in glee as I got ready. "I'm SO keen. You have no idea. This'll be fun. I know where the local sports centre is, and how to get there, I think we should start there in our hunt, but only when I've worked out where the nearest doctor's surgery is."

We walked the now familiar path and headed down the stone steps and across the beach to find the bus that would take us to the local sports centre.

I had googled medical centres and discovered that next to the pool complex was a parade of shops in which there appeared to be both a doctor's surgery and a pharmacy. It struck us that if we went into the chemist shop first and talked to the pharmacist, he or she could advise as to whether we should see a doctor. The pharmacist might even be able to advise as to the best way to get an appointment.

The bus journey was extremely short - just a couple of stops - it took about 10 minutes to get there and both mum and I looked at one another knowingly. We should have walked it. "What have they been saying to us all week?" said mum. "Walk whenever you can."

"Yes, I agree," I said. "We'll walk back."

My excitement about finding the synchro woman had by now mounted to such fever pitch that I would have promised to walk to the moon and back. I was ready to go inside and begin the search. I had the hat tucked into my handbag and mum by my side, looking like a pirate in her large, homemade eyepatch. What could possibly go wrong?

We queued up and waited patiently at the main reception with all the children clutching their towels as they bought tickets for a morning swim.

"I wish I spoke Portuguese," I said to mum. "Even just a few words would make it easier. I don't know how I'm going to explain to this woman what I'm after."

"I was thinking the same thing myself," said Mum. "If she only speaks a few words of English, "synchronised" is unlikely to be one of them."

Once we reached the front of the line, excitement had turned to panic as I realised I was going to have to explain my desires to this woman and there was no doubt that I was going to sound very odd.

"Synchronised swimming," I said, waving the hat around. "Is there anyone here who I can talk to about synchronised swimming?"

The woman looked at me blankly.

"Synchronised swimming," I repeated, as if that was going to help in anyway. Then, the inevitable happened.

"Show me," she said.

"OK," I replied, and began leaping around in the reception in my best interpretation of a synchronised swimmer. I had the fixed smile, the sudden upward jumps and even a few high kicks in order to convey my message. The entire row of children, and most of the people in the café opposite were watching, intrigued by my sudden performance.

Remarkably, the woman on reception seem to understand me.

"Ah," she said. She looked again at the hat and a look of genuine comprehension passed over her face.

"I am understanding now. Down to end on the left. Is there."

"Who is there?" I asked.

"Person of the hat."

"The person who owns this hat is here?" I said. I couldn't believe it. I'd hoped they'd be able to translate the letters on the hat for me, or advise me where to go next, I never expected to be directed straight to Synchro Woman's office.

"Come on," I said. "We're in business."

"Wonderful!" said mum. "And really astonishing that she knew what you wanted from that little routine in reception."

"Cheeky," I said. "That was a magnificent display of floor synchronised swimming, even if I say so myself."

We walked towards the room that we had been directed to

by the lady on reception, when we passed a ladies toilet and mum said she had to go.

"Really? Can you not wait?"

"I'll be two minutes," she insisted

I waited patiently for way more time than is necessary for someone to go to the loo. I had no idea what on earth she was doing in there. I just wanted to go and find the synchronised swimmer. So, I walked down to the room to which the lady had suggested we go, and knocked gently on the door. There was no answer.

"Hello, is anyone there," I said.

I turned the handle cautiously and the door opened onto a small room that looked as if it had been set up for fitness testing. There were scales, callipers and measuring tapes. I slammed the door shut quickly. I didn't need to see callipers and weighing scales. Urgh. It was like a torture chamber in there.

"There you are!" said mum, who had emerged from the ladies toilet and was wandering down the corridor with a familiar-looking woman.

"Look who I found in the ladies," said mum, indicating Tracie standing beside her.

"Hi, how are you doing?" I said. "Have you heard about our mission?"

"Indeed I have," said Tracie. "And I'm going to accompany you. I know exactly where you need to go, follow me…"

And so, the three of us walked confidently through the sports centre, me waddling along, Tracie striding confidently ahead, orange skin gleaming in the sunshine, and mum shuffling along. pirate-style. beside us.

"In here," said Tracie, indicating a door that was nowhere near the one that the receptionist had told us to go to. She knocked gently on it but there was no answer, then she knocked again.

I'll just peek in," she said, turning the handle, but the door wouldn't open.

"Damn, it's locked."

All three of us stood there looking at the locked door for a little while until she had a brainwave.

"I know," she said. She marched off again with the two of us running along behind her, and spoke to a small, tubby woman in Portuguese.

"Follow," said the woman, leading the way through the sports centre. She had an oddly wide gait for someone so small and as she walked, she had her hands resting on her hips. She looked like a cowboy who'd just got off his horse.

"She knows where to go," said Tracie. So, we followed John Wayne through the centre, still in search of the owner of a rather fancy synchronised swimming cap.

The woman led us to an office right back at the back of the building.

"Thank you so much," I said, as she opened the door and talked to a very tall man inside. They had quite a conversation before he said.

"I take you."

So now there were five of us on our mission, walking round the building. The very tall man, the small, fat woman who walked like a cowboy, mum looking like a pirate, me waddling along to keep up, and Tracie with her bright orange, Day-Glo legs.

He took us to another room but that was empty too. Where on earth was this synchro woman? Unfeasibly tall man spoke to Day-Glo legs woman, while cowboy lady watched and nodded. Pirate and I just looked on forlornly. There was lots of shrugging and raised voices.

"No one knows," Tracie said eventually.

"OK," I said, a little confused. "The lady on reception said it was that room at the end of the corridor, right where you come into the centre."

"Oh," said Tracie. "Right - let's go back there then."

So, back we all trouped, through the sports centre, dropping off the man and woman who had accompanied us (but been no use at all), as we went. Then we followed the corridor back and I said: "There, that's the room the lady on reception said was the right one."

"No - that's not right. That's my room."

"Your room? So, you work here?"

"Yes - I do the fitness and nutrition for the squads here."

"Oh. How odd."

"Look, don't worry. We'll find a first aid person somewhere," said Tracie. "They are probably just busy treating someone."

"No - we're not after a medic," I said.

"Yes - for your mother's eye," said Tracie. "I thought that's what you had come for - to find a medical specialist."

"Oh, no, that's my fault," said mum. "I must have confused you when you asked about my eye and I said we were going to find a doctor. We're actually at the sports centre on a rather more complicated mission."

"We are here to ask about synchronised swimming. I found this cap," I said, pulling the swimming hat from my bag.

Tracie practically swooned in front of us and leant heavily against the wall. "Where did you find that?" she said, her eyes wide with excitement.

"It was left by our pool," I said.

"That was your pool?"

"Yes, a lady has been doing synchronised swimming in the pool outside our villa. She left this hat and I wanted to return it to her."

"That's me," said Tracie. "That's my hat."

"It's YOU," both mum and I declared. "Why did you run away when you saw us?"

"I didn't know it was you. I thought you were coming to tell me to get out of your pool, so I got out before you could tell me off."

"We were coming to watch you...you were brilliant."

"Oh," said Tracie, all smiles. "Thank you. That's so sweet."

"How did you learn to do that?"

"It's a long story," said Tracie. "Shall we get some herbal tea?"

"That would be great," I said, hoping I could order a sneaky cappuccino instead. "But first let's go to the pharmacy to get mum sorted, then I want to hear all about this."

The three of us went to the pharmacy around the corner from the sports centre where a very friendly pharmacist said he thought mum's eye was best left alone. He recommended painkillers and some antibacterial eye drops to keep it all as clean as possible, and told her to visit her own GP back in England if it hadn't improved over the next couple of days. He also sold her an eye patch, much to my joy, and recommended regular ice packs and getting lots of rest. Mum nodded gratefully and bought the drugs he advised.

Then it was time to hear Tracie's story.

"I was a very talented synchronised swimmer when I was younger," she said, as we sat sipping some revolting green tea in the cafe near the sports centre (no luck with my attempts to order cappuccino). "I competed for France, then in 1987 I was selected for the World Cup, held in Egypt."

"Oh, my goodness," said mum. "That's amazing. You must be really good."

"I was very good," said Tracie. "But I struggled with terrible stage fright, and I was never very good in the big tournaments. I just froze. That's what I did in the World Cup...I panicked and I fell out of synchro. We were on for medal, and could have won gold, but I messed up and we dropped out of the medals, we came fourth.

"That's the worst place to come...to just miss out on a medal. It was awful. And it was all my fault."

"Oh no," said mum, "I'm sure it wasn't all your fault. It can't have been."

"Yep," said Tracie, nodding vigorously. "All my fault. I did a completely different routine to the others - I just forgot everything."

"You shouldn't beat yourself up," I said, though I did make a mental note to try and find a video of that World Cup - Tracie doing a completely different routine to the rest of the team sounded hysterical. "Fourth in the World Cup is brilliant. The World Cup is probably like the Olympics of synchronised swimming. That's brilliant."

"Yes," mum said. "Really brilliant. Well done."

"Well, it's strange you should mention the Olympics, because they took place the next year," said Tracie, looking even more mournful. "And I was selected. I couldn't believe it. I had another chance."

"Oh, that's fantastic," I said. "I love a story with a happy ending."

"Yeah, except that when I got there, I was so nervous. It was in Seoul and I'd never been anywhere like that before. I was just terrified...and I did exactly the same thing again...I messed up and France missed out on the medals. We came fourth. Again."

"Oh dear, I'm so sorry," said mum. "Really, though - you shouldn't blame yourself. It's quite natural to be nervous performing in front of all those people."

"You're very kind, but it was awful. I stopped the sport as soon as I got back to France and I never did any synchro again...until about two weeks ago. The guys at the sports centre found out about my background and were keen for me to start running synchronised swimmer classes. I froze when they first asked me and said there's no way I could do it, but Rodrigo - the guy in charge here - told me to think about it...and the more I thought about it, the more I thought that I'd actually quite like to do that. But I didn't know whether I could remember anything, so when I came to the camp to give the talks, and saw all those empty pools, I thought I'd come back at night time and have a practice while you were all having dinner. I didn't want to ask anyone in case it drew attention to me. I just wanted a bit of time in the pool by myself to check whether I was still comfortable in the water."

"You certainly looked it," said mum. "You were really impressive when we saw you."

"Thank you," said Tracie. "I loved it. I loved every minute of it, and I'm definitely going to teach lessons at the swimming pool and try and build up a young squad."

"That's amazing," said mum. "I'm so pleased. And I'm sorry if we scared you off when you were practising - we didn't mean any harm at all - we just wanted to watch because you were so good."

I handed the swimming cap over. "Sounds like you're going to need this," I said. "Just one more question - what do the letters inscribed on the inside mean?"

"Oh - they are from my international days - so synchronised swimming in French is nage synchronisée and the 'f' is for France because that's who I was competing for. My name is Tracie Molton, so: NSF/TM is the national team and the swimmer."

"Got it," I said.

Despite mum and I saying that we would walk back, in the end we got a cab with Tracie. She was coming over to join us all for our last evening in camp. We sat comfortably on the back seat and watched the beautiful scenery rush past us.

"That thing in the sports centre was quite funny when you think about it," I said. "You and two senior members of staff in there all joining in the hunt for you."

Tracie smiled. "Yes, that is very funny. I was just asking everyone where the first aid person was."

"I'll miss this place," I said.

"Will you miss all the exercise?" mum asked.

"Nope."

I looked over at Tracie who seemed lost in a world of her own, presumably reliving that moment at the 1988 Olympics when it all went wrong.

"Do you have to do a lot of exercise to lose weight?" I asked. "Only I really do hate it?"

"Yes, Good question," said mum. "And also - which is best - exercising or dieting to lose weight?"

"Well," she said. "You'll be relieved to hear that there's been a study."

"Hooray!" said mum and I.

She laughed. "I'm not that bad, am I? Forever quoting studies."

"No, not bad - it's good," I said quickly. I'm delighted that you've read all these studies."

"Good, well - this was a big study - done in the UK and featuring more than 300,000 patients. The question they asked was: 'Can weight and inactivity be considered separate risks?' In other words - you can exercise and still be fat and you can be thin and not exercise at all. One does not depend on the other.

"So, the study showed that regular exercise will reduce many of the health risks associated with both being over-weight and inactive, but might not directly lead to you losing weight. You have to change your diet to do that.

"This ties in with the other studies that have been done - remember the bus conductor and bus driver study?"

"How could we forget?" I said.

"Well, that was done because drivers were dying earlier, not because they were fatter than conductors. Exercise is important for health and longevity. And you know what else is important?"

"Oooo, do tell," I said.

"The regularity of that exercise. So, if you sit and look at the computer screen for eight hours solid without moving, then go to the gym for an hour, that's not as effective as doing an hour, then some exercise, or having regular exercise breaks through the day. The human body was designed to move."

"So, it would have been ideal if the bus conductors and the drives swapped jobs every hour?" mum said. She can be so wise sometimes.

"Yes - absolutely - that would have saved lives."

"Could it have been stress as well though?" I offer. "I mean - I totally get that exercise is healthy and it's important to build movement into your everyday life, but if I drove a bus all day every day, I'm sure it would be the stress that killed me."

"Back during the bus driver study, stress was not appreciated as a health risk, but you're absolutely right. Things like tight schedules, traffic jams, angry passengers, filthy air and other factors would definitely have been a factor. A life packed with unrelenting stress is far more dangerous than a few extra pounds."

I nodded and smiled, and thanked her for her input, but inside I was thinking 'if I give up work and have no stress in my life, I can eat chocolate all the time.'

CHAPTER EIGHTEEN: WHEN MRS A TURNED UP UNEXPECTEDLY

It was dinner time. Our last dinner of the trip. It had all gone by so quickly. In many ways, I'd absolutely hated it, but in others, I'd loved it. I'd learned so much, and was kind of looking forward to putting it together in the blog posts next week in the hope that it could help other people.

We walked up to the dining room tables and looked around, working out where to sit. "Hey, come and sit by me," Yvonne called out, tapping the seat next to her and causing me to feel all sorts of anxieties. Did she see mum and me crawling through the hotel bar last night, trying to escape without being seen?

"Come on," I said, dragging mum away from where she had stopped to talk to Simon. I noticed he had his hand on her arm as he spoke to her.

For God's sake, will that man never stop?

"Come on mum, come and sit here."

I treated Simon to an angry scowl and indicated to mum where we would be sitting. I took in the shock on her face as she looked at Yvonne and back to me.

"Had a good day?" she said to Yvonne in a rather forced manner.

"Yes, a lovely day thank you. And you?"

"Yes, it's been great," said Mum.

"How's your eye feeling now."

"Much better, thank you. It looks much worse than it feels."

"I didn't see you both this morning," she said to me. "Did you decide to take it easy?"

"I went with mum to find a doctor," I said. "Then we ended up going on a bit of a mission."

Despite promising myself that I would keep my synchronised swimming story to myself, I couldn't help it.

"Oooo...do tell," said Yvonne. I paused my revelations while chef delivered an unbelievably bland looking bowl of what I assume to be soup, but looked like slosh, then continued once he'd left.

"Well there's been this great mystery going on in our villa," I said. "When I got back after the first night, do you remember I went back early because I haven't been very well?"

"Yes, I remember," said Yvonne. "You fell with an almighty thud and we all thought you died."

"I prefer to think of it as me having delicately fainted, but yes – I collapsed. And when I went back to our villa..."

"I need to stop you there," said mum. Will these people ever stop interrupting my story? "You went back to the wrong villa and climbed into Donald's bed."

"Yes, well – after that, when I got back to my villa."

"Hang on, so – the rumours about you and Donald are true? I assumed they weren't..."

"What rumours? No. No. There is definitely nothing going on between me and Donald. I just went back to the wrong villa, went into what I thought was my room and got into bed. That's all."

"And Donald got in beside you?"

"No. I woke up when he came in, and left."

"That's not strictly true, is it?" said mum. "You did stay there for a little bit, and chat to him when he was in the bed."

"No, look – this is all a distraction. Do you want me to tell you my story about what we got up to this morning or not? It's far more interesting than any half-made-up tale about me accidentally going back to the wrong villa."

"Okay, sorry – carry on," said Yvonne. "We can come back to your love affair with Donald later." She nudged mum and they both giggled at this point but I was determined not to be thrown.

"Well, anyway, when I got back to my room on the first night, the room felt really stuffy, so I opened the patio windows."

Are you sure you weren't just all hot and bothered from your night of passion with Donald?" said Mum.

"No, I was hot because my roommate had forgotten to put the air-conditioning on."

"Oh yes," said Mum. "I just thought it was such a waste of money to leave the air-conditioning on when we were there. It hadn't occurred to me that it would be like a sauna when we got back."

I glared at mum, but Yvonne put her arm round her conspiratorially and said, "It's an easy mistake to make. Almost easy as accidentally getting into a man's bed."

"Can I carry on with my story now?"

"Yes, go on dear," said Mum.

"When I stepped outside and wandered towards the pool, I could see there was a woman in there doing synchronised swimming."

"What?" said Yvonne. "That's so weird… How could there have been someone in there doing synchronised swimming?"

"I know! It was very odd. I sat on the edge of the sun lounger for a while, just watching, but when I moved closer to the pool, the woman saw me and swam like a mad thing towards the edge, climbed out and ran away into the trees. I stood up, and went to go after her, but she'd disappeared."

"I thought she'd gone completely mad," said mum. "You know these people who collapse and have a bang on the head and then are never quite the same afterwards? We thought that's what had happened to Mary."

"I knew I was right though," I said. "I watched for five or 10 minutes, and she was really good, I definitely hadn't imagined it."

"Okay, so what happened next?" said Yvonne. I'd obviously piqued her interest.

"The same thing happened the next night, and again I was on my own, and when I told mum she thought I must have lost my mind. But then last night mum was with me and we saw the swimmer again in the pool."

"Oh, and she was wonderful," said mum. "Very beautiful, gliding through the water in the moonlight she looked like someone in the Olympics you know with a sudden spring up out of the water with a mad smile? She was doing all of that."

I explained to Yvonne how we walked over to stand near the pool, to get a better look, and the swimmer saw us and fled again, but this time she left behind her swimming cap and inside were these initials..."'

Just as I was about to continue with the story, Yvonne's phone buzzed into action, and she looked down at it where there was a text message.

"I'm so sorry, I'm dying to hear the end of your story, but I have to go, can you tell me all about it at breakfast?"

"Sure," I said, glancing at mum who immediately looked at me. "I'll tell you the end of the story in the morning."

"Okay, I'll see you then. Sorry to run out. Have a lovely evening."

With that, she was gone, speeding out of the villa.

I looked at mum. "Well I think we know where she's going," I said. "She must be going to meet him again. You can't tell me that she suddenly, desperately, felt the urge to have a sauna."

"No, you're right dear," said Mum.

"And, by the way - stop mentioning the whole Donald thing. Nothing happened it was a simple mistake."

"OK," said mum. "And actually synchronised swimming woman didn't even come that first night, did she? It was the night afterwards. You only saw her once before I was with you. You're losing your mind. I'm the old one – you're supposed to be the one with a good memory."

As we sat there looking at one another, we saw Staff A leave. He walked nonchalantly out of the room then ran up the stone steps, turning a sharp left at the top.

"Do you think we should follow them again?" I said to mum. "It worked out so well last time."

"Ha, ha," she said. "Which bit of it did you think worked out well then?"

"You know the one thing that confuses me about their affair - why aren't they sneaking back to his room? Why would they run off like that, then just sit in a bar? It seems crazy."

"Yes, that is odd," said mum. "Unless they have a room in the hotel?"

"Oh yes. That's probably what they're up to. Oh, go on. Let's follow them again. It's such fun," I said. "I get a real thrill from it. Today was hysterical - finding Tracie. I can't believe how that happened."

As mum and I sat there chatting, a middle-aged woman appeared in the doorway with an overnight bag, looking around, confused. She was wasn't anyone I recognised from the course, and she didn't look as if she worked at the villa.

"Hello, are you looking for Abi?" I said.

As I spoke, Abi came out of the kitchen and saw the lady.

"Anne!" she cried. "How lovely to see you, I didn't realise you were coming."

The two women hugged warmly and she put down her bag.

"I wasn't planning to, but I thought I'd surprise him. I thought we could spend the evening together."

"Oh, he will be delighted," said Abi. "I'm not sure where he is actually. Let me see if I can find out."

Abi disappeared, and Anne sat herself down at a table near the door.

"How are you feeling then, now we're at the end of the week. We managed to get through it all, with only a few minor disasters," said mum.

"OK. I actually quite enjoyed it in the end. Except for boxing. Dad's going to have a fit when he sees your eye," I said.

"I know. I have warned him what to expect when he picks us up at the airport."

As we talked, Abi came up to us. "Have you seen Staff A?" she asked.

I looked at mum and we both looked back at her.

"I think he might have gone out for a walk," I said eventually.

Neither of us wanted to lie, but neither of us wanted to say where he was either, in case he wasn't supposed to be there.

Anne stood up from the table, and walked over to join us.

"This is Anne, Staff A's wife," she said.

"Ohhhh!" I said.

"Nice to meet you," mum said, in a much more controlled fashion.

Then Simon walked over. "I think he's gone down to the hotel bar by the seafront," he said. "He pops down there most evenings to catch up with friends."

"Are you sure?" I said. "He's probably not. He's probably just in his room."

"No – he's not in his room – I just checked," said Abi. "I needed to ask him something, but he's not there. Let me get my jacket, and we'll walk down to the seafront and take a look," Abi said to Anne. "I'll just be a minute."

"You could phone the bar," I suggested. "No need to go down there."

"No – we'll walk. It's a lovely evening."

Abi went to get her jacket and I looked at mum.

"Shall we go," I said to her, while grabbing my hoodie, nodding at Anne, and speed walking towards the door.

"Where are we going?" said mum, running to catch up with me.

"We have to warn them," I said. "We can't let his wife walk in on them."

"OK, you go ahead. My laces are undone. I'll do them up and be right behind you."

I ran ahead of mum, and bolted down the street. Somehow, I was given speed and strength by the mission to get to the amorous lovers before Anne. I ran like the wind - across the gravelly paths and over the grass verges, then down towards the seafront bar on a mission to save a man's marriage.

CHAPTER NINETEEN: THE TRUTH ABOUT YVONNE

I burst into the bar and there sat Staff A and Yvonne, holding hands over the table, and looking at one another adoringly.

"Hey," I screamed as I fell towards their table, barely able to talk after all that running. "Move apart, move apart," I shouted. "She'll be here any minute."

Everyone in the bar looked up as I confronted them. I was red in the face and sweating profusely as I started physically manhandling Staff A in an effort to move him away from Yvonne.

"Mary what on earth's the matter?" I couldn't move him. I was panting like a wild animal on a hunt.

"Your wife. She's here," I spluttered, motioning between Staff and Yvonne. I noticed they hadn't stopped holding hands so I leaped in and yanked their hands apart. "For the love of God - do I have to do everything?" I asked, as I saw mum and Mrs A coming into the bar.

"Your wife," I said dramatically, sweeping my hand back to indicate her arrival, before I whispered to Yvonne. "You better run. Quick. It's his wife."

"Hi Anne," said Yvonne, getting up and hugging the woman. "Have you met Mary?" she said.

"Very briefly," said Anne, nodding in my direction.

"Is everything OK?" said a man from the table next to us. I looked up to tell him that everything was fine, when he recognised me. "It's you," he said. "The woman from last night - the one who flashed her bottom at everyone in the sauna and crawled out of the bar on her hands and knees. I'm amazed you have the cheek to show your face in here again."

"What?" said Staff A.

"Oh, it's nothing, nothing at all. Mistaken identity," I said.

The man saw mum standing there and gasped. "My goodness - what happened to your eye?"

"Oh that? That's nothing," said mum. "Mary punched me in the face, but it's much better now."

"Punched you in the face? What sort of animal are you?" he asked me.

"Look, it's fine," said Staff A, standing up and putting his hand out to show the man he wanted him to back off. "I can deal with this."

"You need to run, Quickly," I whispered to Yvonne. "Go now. Save yourself."

The man went back to his table, and Staff A pulled over a couple of chairs

"Take a seat," he said. "Let me get you a drink."

"Oooo. A drink? What - a proper drink?"

"Yes, I'll get you a proper drink. What do you want?"

I ordered a large glass of wine and sat back in anticipation. Mum said she'd have a cup of tea. Yvonne got up and walked to the bar with Staff A while mum, Mrs A and I sat there in horrible, painful silence.

"OK, so what's this all about? Why have you come charging

down here and attempted to pull me out of my seat? And what's all this about you flashing everyone in the sauna?" asked Staff A, handing me my drink.

I decide not to address the sauna incident. "To be honest, I thought you and Yvonne were having an affair and when your wife arrived in camp, I thought I ought to come down here before her to warn you. Although, I'm guessing that's not what's going on here, is it?"

Staff A exploded into rip-roaring laughter, and put his arm around me in a friendly fashion. "Oh Mary, you are funny. Yvonne's half my age and I've been happily married for 30 years. My God, this woman has stuck with me through thick and thin, I'm not about to mess her around now."

He and Anne held hands and looked at one another.

"But you've been secretly meeting every night, and you said you didn't know Yvonne when you picked her up at the airport, so I knew you weren't friends...I suppose I just assumed..."

"I didn't say that I didn't know her - I said that I'd never met her before. Look, even though I've never met her, I feel like I know her so well because her dad talked about her all the time."

He trailed off at this point, and looked at Yvonne. "Do you mind if I tell them," he said.

"No, that's fine," said Yvonne. "I don't mind at all."

"OK, well I've been in jail for the past six months. I was locked up after an incident in Afghanistan. I was accused of mistreatment of prisoners...something I never did. It was a horrible time. I was accused of things that no one wants to be accused of."

"Waterboarding?" I asked, remembering Staff B's reaction when I had used the word in jest. "Was it something to do with that?"

"I'm not going into any details, Mary. If you read that in

the press then I would ignore anything else that you read in the press about me because I was cleared of everything."

"No - I didn't read anything in the press," I said. "Honestly."

"OK, well the facts are that I was found guilty and locked up, but then evidence emerged which proved that I didn't do it, indeed couldn't have done it. That's all I'm saying. I was freed three weeks ago and didn't go back into the army.

"While I was in prison, there was a guy there who saved my life. He kept me strong, and urged me to keep up the appeal. He was Yvonne's dad. I said that when I came out, I would meet up with her and check she was OK. Then I got this job, and it seemed like the perfect job for me. But I wanted to see Yvonne, so I thought the best thing would be to get Yvonne to come out here. We've been meeting so I can tell her all about her dad in prison."

"Oh," I said. "Gosh, I'm really sorry. I didn't know - I was just trying to help, you know. I didn't want Anne to walk in on you. I just...sorry…"

"It's fine," said Yvonne. "I would have told you all about it if you'd asked."

"Oh," I said, turning to mum. "I never thought about asking. Did you?

Mum shook her head and finished her tea.

"Shall we go back," I said. "Leave these good people to talk."

"Yes," said mum. "I think that's probably for the best. We've done enough interfering for one day. We need to pack, we have an early flight in the morning."

"OK, see you both before you leave," said Staff A.

"You won't be up that early, will you?" said mum. "We have to leave at 7.30am to get our flight."

"Yes - I'll be up. I'm weighing you first thing, remember. We'll see how much weight you've lost."

"Oh yes - how exciting," said mum. "I'm dying to find out."

"Yeah," I said, really regretting the sneaky coke, crisps and jelly babies and Mars bars (OK - I didn't mention the Mars bars and jelly babies but I knew you'd judge me harshly if I did).

CHAPTER TWENTY: FINAL RESULTS

I stood before the scales like an Olympian about to step up to the start line in the Olympic 100m final. The only difference was that this athlete knew she'd been cheating...sneakily eating and drinking through the week when people weren't watching: coke, crisps, Mars bars and jelly babies. I know, I know - it's terrible, and I'd only cheated myself, but I couldn't have survived on the rations they gave us. Honestly, I'd be dead now. Dead. And the staffs would be up for murder. Would they want that on their consciences? No, they wouldn't. Their lives would be ruined by it. I was doing them a favour by eating; saving them from misery and guilt.

In any case I knew I had eaten far less than I usually would, and exercised a tonne more but still - I couldn't possibly have lost more than a few pounds.

I'd sat there as others in the group had lost up to 6lbs. I knew I'd be looking at 2lbs at the most. I was hit by a sudden rush of disappointment in myself, and anger that I hadn't done this properly...just for four days, to see how much weight I could lose. But then there was the whole 'I might die' thing.

Maybe this was better.

"On you pop then," said Staff A, like this was some sort of fun adventure I was engaging in.

I stepped onto the scales and watched the numbers whizz up...17 stone, 18 stone, 19 stone...then it slowed down. It stopped just before 20 stone. "You're 19 stone 9lbs," said Staff. I looked at him as if he'd taken leave of his senses.

"That's insane," I said.

"It's pretty good going, Mary. You've lost 9lbs. You're our biggest loser. Well done! Your mum lost 5lbs and you've lost nine, that's a whole stone between you."

There was a ripple of applause behind me and a small shriek of excitement from mum and they presented me with a floral headdress bearing the words 'biggest loser'.

"Thank you," I said. "This has been the most glorious and interesting trip ever."

I turned to Staff A and gave him a big hug and said something I never thought I'd say: "Thank you for pushing me and believing in me."

"Any time," he said.

Mum and I hugged everyone before leaving, then Staff B came out to our cab with us, carrying our bags.

"You're a superstar," I said, hugging him tightly. "Thanks for your support."

"It's been a pleasure," I said. "We're all really looking forward to reading your blog."

"Ha, ha," I said. "Then you'll know exactly what I got up to."

"Indeed," said Staff B, closing the door for us and giving a mock salute as the car drove off.

"When does your blog go up?" asked mum.

"In two days' time," I said. "When I'm safely out of the country."

"What are you going to write in it?"

"I'm going to write about everything," I said. "Every last

detail, but mainly I'm going to say how brilliant it was, and how much I learned. It was brilliant, wasn't it?"

"It was fantastic," said mum, giving me a gentle hug. "Thank you for taking me."

"It's a pleasure. I'm so glad you came. I'm never eating carrots again. Not ever."

"Nor me," said mum. "nor me."

Ends

I HOPE YOU ENJOYED THE BOOK!

If you want to learn more about Bernice Bloom (and if you want a free book!), go to: www.bernicebloom.com. And if you enjoyed the book and could leave me a review, that would be brilliant! x

There are loads more books in the Adorable Fat Girl series & lots more being released all the time.

Books in the series that are OUT NOW:

CLICK ON THE LINKS BELOW FOR MORE DETAILS:

UK: https://www.amazon.co.uk/Bernice-Bloom/e/B01MPZ5SBA/ref=dp_byline_cont_ebooks_1

US: https://www.amazon.com/Bernice-Bloom/e/B01MPZ5SBA/ref=dp_byline_cont_ebooks_1

Is romance your thing?

If it is, see my new romantic novels under the pen name, Rosie Taylor-Kennedy - I've written a series of books about four sisters who live together in Sunshine Cottage in a beautiful village called 'Cove Bay.' It's like Little Women for the modern reader! See here for more details:

https://www.amazon.co.uk/Return-Sunshine-Cottage-Bernice-Bloom-ebook/dp/B07GXY3Y98/ref=asap_bc?ie=UTF8

RETURN TO SUNSHINE COTTAGE
BERNICE BLOOM
ROSIE TAYLOR-KENNEDY

LIFE AT SUNSHINE COTTAGE
BERNICE BLOOM
ROSIE TAYLOR-KENNEDY

GIRLS AT SUNSHINE COTTAGE
BERNICE BLOOM
ROSIE TAYLOR-KENNEDY

MEMORIES OF SUNSHINE COTTAGE
BERNICE BLOOM
ROSIE TAYLOR-KENNEDY

And there are lots more books on the way, including Mary's Road Trip to USA with Ted and another mystery for Mary to solve, called Adorable Fat Girl and the Mysterious Pregnancy, and Confessions of an Adorable Fat Girl out this summer...

Then there's the relaunch of a very funny series of books about Wags... all coming over the next few months.

See the website here: www.bernicebloom.com AND make sure you come and join the Facebook group, full of great, fun women: https://www.facebook.com/BerniceBloombooks/?tn-str=k*F

** Thank you so much for all your support **

Printed in Great Britain
by Amazon